A LATE NIGHT FRIGHT

TALES OF HORROR AND MACABRE

VEDANT SRIVASTAVA

Dedication

Dedicated to my parents, without whose blessings this book would not have happened.

To my lovely sister, who annoys me to no extent.

To Sarah, Alina and Andy; wouldn't have named you guys if I had any other friends.

To my relatives who backed the writing of this book. Now read it.

Author Bio

When not swimming with the nightmares, he can be found running with the horrors. **Vedant Srivastava** was born in the ancient city of Varanasi, India, which allowed him to witness the supernatural and spiritual connect of the humanity closely. That, alongside a steady diet of horror books and his mother's fairytales, influenced his early years. Though, the author admits he saw Evil Dead movie entirely too young and that was a big mistake. Regaled with horror stories since childhood, this is the author's attempt at weaving some new terrors of his own; and for the first time in English language.

Content Warning:

This book may contain creative depictions of death, self-harm and mental health issues; in addition to good old-fashioned scares and spooks.

Contents

Preface

"The process of delving into the black abyss is to me the keenest form of fascination."
- H. P. Lovecraft

My fascination with horror goes back to days of Goosebumps books and t.v. series. I should give an honorable mention to the Indian 'It' remake, whose Pennywise burned the earliest memories of terror in my mind. With the right mix of horror stories told to me, comics and horror shows watched alone (with front door open, in case I needed to bail), the cocktail for creating monsters and terrors had already started to brew early in my childhood.

Then, teenage and a personal phone with internet came along and a world full of horrors opened up. Lovecraft, King, Shelley, Poe, Creepypasta? Yes please! Soon, I realized there was more to horrors than the usual possessions and monsters. The crux of horror no longer lay in its ability to scare me, but in the ability to bring something new and unorthodox to the table.

This thought has since made me appreciate horror movies and stories more, particularly the ones that failed to bring performance or scares to the table, but brought concepts so weird, so uncomfortable or so unsettling and out of this world, that it makes me stop, take notice and smile.

But you are reading this to find out what to expect going ahead! Starting with influences, my main influences in horror story writing are H. P. Lovecraft, for his cosmic horror is my first love and Stephen King, for the wild unorthodox concepts he comes up with; right alongside R. L. Stine's use of teen humor. Edgar Allen Poe's The Gold Bug was my first treasure hunt story and The Raven was a masterpiece that permanently imprinted on me.

I must add some untraditional sources – Thanks to my schooling, I was exposed to the descriptive short story styles of H. H. Munro and Munshi Premchand. I also cannot forget reading for the first time, works of William Sydney Porter, who was a magician of words with his surprise endings and his descriptions of surrounding environment. Beautiful and calming depictions of nature in Robert Frost's poems have had a huge impact on me. Rabindra Nath Tagore's works deserve special praise too.

Hence, you will find a few references in following stories, written deliberately as homage or ode to some lesser-known but legendary stories. That is my attempt at writing a love letter to the beautiful works of Lovecraft and others.

Moving onto philosophy, I have always found that allure of horror is literally in the unknown. Thus, I firmly believe in the saying that **"Your nightmares can always come true, you just have to be unlucky enough."** There is no rhyme or reason to supernatural and there is no explaining it. And as such, a horror can happen to anyone, anywhere, anytime, one just has to be unfortunate!

I believe 'horrors' don't owe a joyful ending to any of us; they owe us conclusions to their endings but not necessarily happy endings or resolutions. They need not provide any reason, background or backstory to us but "the story" itself and a good conclusion, that makes us gasp, makes us ponder and leaves us asking for more or feeling empty. This philosophy has ruled my mind and stayed with me as I discover new books, movies and video games.

In my stories I have tried to cover my favorite themes of horror; from cosmic horror to surprise endings, the madness, the undefined and the supernatural entities from beyond and their games against us puny mortals. I have been charmed by the magic of my idols and I hope you can be charmed by what you unearth in the following pages.

I must now fade away and let you explore, before you break free of my hypnotizing rants. Happy screaming!

Vedant Srivastava

Capture The Moment

crunch crunch

The first time we see Emma, making her way down the street. Her boots making the crunching sound on the fresh snow, the best thing about the season.

8.30 P.M. Her watch declared. It's darker than usual tonight.

There were just two stragglers on the street far away, hurrying to their destination unknown. Even though they had passed her a minute ago, she could still make out their silhouettes clearly in the snow.

She was all alone. But she could not be bothered. She crossed her arms into her parka tightly. Lucky her, she had prepared for the winds before leaving.

crunch crunch

Emma kept on walking, she felt like she should hum a song, maybe that will beat the loneliness. Sadly no, her dark lips weren't ready to brave the cold apparently.

Emma was no average girl or at least she believed so. She fit in everywhere, she was accepted everywhere she went. Yet activity drained her, and loneliness was a welcome break she always knew she needed. She was the perfect introvert.

If one looked closely, they could see a faint twinkling in her eyes, of dreams and hopes, of loss and regrets and more so of expectations and responsibilities. Behind the side bangs, her dark lipstick, her eyeshadow lay a tale of missed opportunities and lost chances.

She looked ahead at the desolate street. The sodium lamps lit the empty sidewalks at fixed distances, alternating between light and darkness. "Perfectly balanced." She smiled like she had cracked a brilliant philosophical joke.

crunch crunch

Her shoes announced, as they pressed the snow deeper into the ground.

Skraaaaaaaaaaatch

Breaking the rhythm of her steps, came a new sound. It was a loud tearing sound as if someone tore a plastic wrap on loudspeakers. The sound momentarily bellowed through the night sky and was gone in an instant, like nothing had ever happened. Emma looked up and around. Then she looked back.

Wait?!?!

She stopped.

She could still see those two men, walking away at a distance. 'Curious.' she thought. 'They should have been further away by now.' She shrugged, having spent her miniscule attention span already and started moving again.

She crossed the road and by now she was walking next to the city park. The road was still empty. The city was dead and the night was alive. All she had to accompany her were the darkness, the loneliness, the guilt but also the soft fresh snow that kissed her hair and the chilly wind that pinched her ribs like needles. That, and those two passersby.

'Who were they?' 'What was their story?' 'What brought them

out tonight on these dead roads in this weather?' she wondered. A curiosity that will never be satisfied. The figures still were barely visible but that didn't bother her anymore. Emma was glad she had some company. Just three creatures under the same dark sky.

Suddenly, there was a mild shaking, as if earth itself tried waking up from slumber and then went back to sleep.

"Great. An earthquake is just what I need to top my night off." she said, frowning. She regained her balanced and off she went ahead, to her destination unknown.

She was so unbothered, that she barely noticed a man curiously standing and looking at her from across the street.

crunch crunch

Her boots crunching the snow and the whistling winds were the only sounds breaking the eerie silence that lay heavy on these late hours.

Emma was used to being unbothered by distractions, incurious and unafraid. Yet enough oddities had happened tonight to give her a feeling of unease. Her shoes ploughed through the snow as she picked up the pace. Her grip got tighter around the parka, her nails almost digging into it.

Instinctively she turned around, and lo, two tiny figurines were still visible, walking away from her yet the distance never increasing.

A sense of dread overtook her. That's when her fears guided her sight to the man across the street. The man himself was at a distance, standing still but looking at her intently.

Standing slightly out of reach of the nearest street lamp's coverage, the diffused light was adequate to mark out his outlines in an overcoat. The face was not visible in the shadows that engulfed him, neither were any other features. However, in front of him was a small stand with a thin frame that reminded Emma of a painter's easel.

Emma realized she had frozen in terror, and turned around to immediately move away. Her face showed panic. The winds suddenly started picking up to match her frantic rush towards safety.

At that very moment, another powerful tremor erupted, throwing Emma off her balance as she fell face first into the concrete.

***

"Wait a second, hold on." Liz said.

"WHAT ARE YOU DOING YOU FOO… Pardon madame?" the tiny man turned to Liz, his face turning red from embarrassment.

"What is it, mademoiselle?" he inquired.

"Oh, nothing. I thought the painting moved." Liz answered sheepishly.

"It is very moving, yes? La meilleure qualité!" the man replied with the widest grin. His annoyed workers looked at Liz, probably blaming her for wasting their time as they packed the painting.

"I meant it looked like something moved… Never mind." Liz said but she bit her lips before she could say something sillier.

"But madame, then you just keep the doors closed. If it still goes somewhere, we don't refund." he broke off in the wildest fit of laughter.

'What an odd joke from an equally odd person!' Liz remarked internally. 'This guy is so out of era that he would be right at home fleecing Abraham Lincoln out of his money for some paintings.'

She gave one last look at the plastic wrapped painting as it was lowered into a thin wooden crate by the workers who were taking extreme precautions to smoothly lower it down for a third and hopefully final time.

Liz was touched by the odd beauty, a lone melancholy girl walking all alone in the snowfall and two shadows in a distant background. There was something about the pain and sadness of the painting that she related to on a deep level.

She felt oddly connected with the painting. The apartments behind the park in the background seemed familiar. She reasoned that it was definitely based off the local city park. She hadn't been there since she was a teen herself. And she would never, considering it was notorious ever since some people went missing a few years ago.

"Would you like to see anything else madame?" the man said, breaking her chain of thoughts.

"No thank you! You did all of these yourself? Must be a very busy man," she pointed at the display hall where every inch was adorned with the finest piece of art. "I like your style, very realistic!"

"Merci beaucoup madame, you are too kind. I like to, how do you say, um, *capture the entire moment?*"

"Capture the moment. Hmm." Liz repeated under the breath. "You don't know what it means do you?"

Apparently, he must have heard her muttering because the man's demeanor changed suddenly to something otherworldly, before it quickly returned to normal and with his regular French accent he responded jokingly, "No madame, I do not!"

"That will be all. Thanks again." Liz sheepishly replied as she walked out, seeing that the workers had finished loading the painting in the truck. 'It will go above my bed.' The thought made her happy.

On her way out, she looked at a few paintings. There was a painting of some 16th century American settlers' village. The word "CROATOAN" prominently carved inside and above the painting. Next was a weird looking ship, with metal frames around it. The painting was labelled "USS Cyclops". She did not know what any of that meant. *A quick search on internet would have revealed a very curious history of people and ship that had gone missing.*

'Highly uninteresting.' Liz smirked, unimpressed by the display, and walked out.

A Horror Ten Times Ten

"That is not dead which can eternal lie, and in strangest aeons even death may die."
- H. P. Lovecraft

My past attempts at proving my sanity have only succeeded in inviting the most brilliant men in the field of brain disorders to unanimously agree to have me committed to the asylum. My most vehement beliefs refuted as mere ramblings of a madman. Even a cruel perverse mind, they said, can only come up with half the ingenious ideas that I claim are the truth. Over the time, however, I have learnt the art of keeping to myself and refuting my own facts, lest they send me away for good.

I have spent the better part of the last two years adamantly insisting my innocence regarding the horrors that befell the local community and my friend, Jasper Smith, of the Smiths descending from one of the old original families of New England.

The horrors, though real, are very utterly fantastic to the commoners and gentry alike and hence were subjected to ridicule. No amount of conviction can bring forth the sheer understanding required to understand my predicament.

I fear I am still under the suspicion and the eye of the law, if only due to the condition of the scene as discovered and the gruesome event that happened, of which I was the sole survivor along with my aforementioned friend, who was found in a delirious state of mind.

Confounding everyone due to its fantastic imaginative connotations, and worse still, the similar circumstances in which another set of events happened in the same pattern five years ago in a town of Ireland, it too with a sole survivor, the events have piqued many an interest in certain quarters studying the occult.

I can no longer take this insult or be subjected to hateful and curious glances. I must speak up for the final time, and depart from this world without awaiting the judgment and responses of the general public, who anyway have no desire to accept the lurking cosmic horrors right beyond their sight. I will end my life and my travails after this.

I must clarify the circumstances which saw me arriving breathless after my flight from the community, or where the inhabitants of the settlement are, and why my great friend was found in a state of delirium and has never recovered since.

***

When one goes towards Fort Adams, taking a wrong turn on the Ridge Road in the city of Newport, Rhode Island, one comes across a slate gray-colored mansion of old style facing the sea over the cliffs, led from rows of twenty three tiny houses in a very small community of a mere hundred people, mostly of Irish, British and a few of Spanish ancestries. It was served by a telegraph station and an inn, which was a place for gatherings and drinks for visitors from nearby communities and weary travelers alike.

The road, once in its heyday, was a major means of local commerce until the ferry service bypassed it. Now the travelers are few and far between and the inn just rots, its fortunes having departed long ago with the ferry launch.

When my friend purchased the deed to the mansion, he instantly took up the chance to build his base and invited me to join him, if only on the pretext for me to have some cold seaside air for my lungs and help him with the renovations, which he had already started before my arrival.

This act, however, was met with much consternation and hatred, as opposed to the initial warm welcome and joyous reaction on accounts of new avenues of employment and commerce for locals, because the superstitious New England folks still believed in the curse plaguing the land before the mansion was built, its subsequent evacuation overtime and its fall of reputation from peak. They feared the reappearance of a long-forgotten curse, a sentiment, however, not much popular among the youth.

After basic repair works on the pillars and courtyard and redecoration of the inner quarters, extensive work began on rebuilding the foundations on the cliffside. Much to the surprise of all, it started emptying its guts of archaeological marvels, ranging from native Indian objects to intricately carved Spanish treasure boxes. The images gave vivid details of human sacrifice, burials and Spanish inquisitions.

Of them, most curious were the as yet unidentified site and

stones that could not be traced back to anyone but had been in worship back from certain unknown tribes, all the way to natives, the first settlers, then Spaniards and down to modern day cults, none of which, save the natives, were ever known to be present or seen there.

Jasper assured me his motives were purely monetary in nature and he had every intention of selling these to the highest paying collecting party. He was not interested in preservation of any culture.

I settled in nicely. My host kindly provided me with a corner room, with a balcony facing the courtyard and three windows facing the community street, the sea and the courtyard respectively.

The living quarters were located on the first floor, its entrance through a stone-built corridor and the servant's quarters just beyond mine. The corridor had a heavy splintering oak door which opened into the grand hall.

It is here my nightmares started...

On the very first night, two nights prior to a full moon night, I lay in my bed. The moon was singing to me, its lights dancing on my face. Calling me.

And then I woke up!

Startled. Sweating. I was dreaming? It was surreal. As I lay in my bed, continuing to ponder ... I heard it.

Footsteps.

Footsteps in the corridor.

Mild scraping on the floor.

skrish skrash

I tiptoed to my door. Holding it silently ajar I peered into the darkened corridor.

Nothing.
Suddenly a looming shadow towered over me!
I gasped.
Then I heaved a sigh of relief.
It was the cook.
The fat French cook!

'Goodness. I am tired', I remarked to myself. I tried to return to my sleep but something hit my weary senses once more.
I listened.
It was a drum beat!
A faint and muffled drum beat.
thump
thump
thump

Single beat, smooth, nearly inaudible and ethereal. The beats were evenly spaced and took their time. I tried, but alas - I could not pin the source. It could be from either the bowels of the mansion that were full of rubble, or in the forest that lay beyond the courtyard - I knew not.

I stood there watching, listening and to my amazement I noted the cook was dancing to it! His rhythmic movements - timed to the beats. A ridiculous dance if any. He repeated the same patterns again and again.

Head bowed, back hunched, both hands clasped behind his back obediently, like a child.
He was swaying his body this way, and his feet did the dancing.
Left foot twirl around to left
Step forward with right foot
Left foot twirl around to left
Step forward with right foot

Bow
Right foot twirl around to right
Step forward with left foot
Right foot twirl around to right
Step forward with left foot
Bow

This was madness! Did he consume too much ale tonight? Is he sick? Is he happy?

Is this some infernal conjuror's ritual?

Is he celebrating some forgotten festival of a bygone era? Some modern cultist's observance of unmentionable dark practices, as it has been the latest plague reported from murkier corners of port towns?

Between my ponderings, he had already reached the oak door at the end of the corridor where the oil lamps provided better light. The oak door, nearby stone walls and paintings were drenched in yellow lights, while the rest of the corridor slept in darkness and moonlight occasionally lit it from spaced windows.

I saw his face. In the yellow light, half covered by darkness, half illuminated. No expressions. Eyes shut. But a faint smile among his curled lips.

And I realized... He... HE WAS SLEEPING!!!

I instinctively shut my door, afraid he might wake up from his damned sleep walk and see me watching with curiosity. Being the short-tempered man he is, I did not want my morning omelet to be destroyed in vengeance by Pierre.

Before I noticed, I was back in the embrace of sleep.

***

The next morning, I woke up heavy-headed and a full hour late. After my routine I made my way straight for breakfast and to meet my friend. I noted Jasper too had red eyes, a sign of poor sleep and the breakfast had not been served.

"Pierre is nowhere to be found." he fumed.

Our cook was missing, and caused a lot of grief and anger to my very busy friend, not wanting to be taken aback by minor inconveniences.

Our kind young maid, a frolicking country girl of nineteen, gladly set up tables and made some breakfast, lamenting all the while that it was unusual for our cook to leave unannounced, to which Jasper agreed, having kept the cook in his employment for the past many years.

I decided not to speak up of the horrors of last night, as I was unsure whether it had been a genuine sight or a trickery of nefarious dreams, brought about by a cold damp room.

After a brisk breakfast, we buried ourselves in further digging at cliffside foundations, where the facade bowels poured even more curious tablets and artworks.

A closer reading of the pictures and my studies over the past two years have helped me generate a clear and better visual of those hellish, devious, unholy artifacts' importance, that I must briskly add as a gist to keep the cause of the horror relevant.

As per those objects, a cult of bygone era had existed there since man first set foot in the region, worshiping curious "star spawns", "visitors of moonlight", "terror beyond tongue", "drum beater of cosmos", "the king of many faces" among other names.

The cult itself was adept in converting and adapting deviants of new settlers that arrived over generations. These new adherents, each more zealous than their predecessors, kept their faith in the privacy of dark dungeons and dense green forest where no man dared enter.

They had done so from the times of natives, and had continued beyond white settlers, Spanish Baptists and Irish immigrants.

At all times these deviants themselves were reviled by their own communities, sometimes even persecuted, keeping traditions alive by holding their unholy rituals in dark forest and hidden burrows, dancing naked in the full moon. Cannibalism and sacrifices abounded as offerings to their visitors from the stars.

After the proper cataloging of these precious artifacts and putting them under lock and key, we had a proper meal made by our maid, for the cook had not returned and we had no more hopes. Then after a brief chat, we retired for the night.

***

I was so tired from working and studying the artifacts that I had not cared about the previous night's events. Of course, I had never considered that the terror might return again.

Later in the night, I was at my study desk by the balcony door, finishing the letter to my beloved when I first heard it.
thump
thump
thump
A faint drum. It had returned!

Taken aback once more, and with much curiosity, I listened

intently for the source, rather unsuccessfully, as the drums appeared to be coming from a cliff, forest or beyond the town with same intensity.

I ran into the balcony, flushed with pale light from the waxing gibbous moon, and looked around. But before I could find the source of the unearthly drum beatings, my eyes fell on something more chilling. How I wish I had evaded that sight. *It was a shadow.*

An awkwardly moving figure. It was a person. In our courtyard! The shadow person limped to the center of the yard over dimly shining marbles.

I watched in anticipation for the big reveal as the corner of the courtyard's wall had some lanterns lit. My heartbeat rose and my breath choked in my lungs. Perspiration came out - on a cold night.

Any moment now.

Nothing in my wildest imagination could have prepared me for the shock and wild horror of revelation of such a simple identity, yet it shook me to my core and horrified me. *It was the maid!*

She moved silently, but even in dim light I could tell her white maid's bonnet, her dirty dull pink frock. She was swaying at the infernal beastly music coming out of ether. Back hunched, hands clasped behind her, head dropped low.

thump

Left foot twirl around to left

thump

Step forward with right foot

thump

Left foot twirl around to left

thump
Step forward with right foot
thump
Bow
thump
Right foot twirl around to right
thump
Step forward with left foot
thump
Right foot twirl around to right
thump
Step forward with left foot
thump
Bow
Again, the dance in circles.
Again, the slow repetitive beats.
Again, in sequence of ten.
Why ten?

I thought I momentarily saw the light in my friend's chamber lit, or I must be imagining it. I could no longer tell the real world apart from my dream world under the moon.

I don't remember much of the next chain of happenings, but I do remember waking up late in the morning on my balcony. I must have passed out due to the terror of what I had witnessed...

It is where I had seen the horror, something so inexplicable but purely mind numbing, something at which I fainted, that it would surely be taken as a jest to be mentioned in the same breath as horror by anyone who hadn't witnessed the events of that night.

I peeked a glance at her face... Pure, pale, young, eyes closed, lips curled into a smile. She was asleep!

But behind her, in the thickets at the periphery of property, stood shadows. Still, motionless, breathless. It was a great crowd of humans, facing me but expressionless, as if they too were sleeping…

***

Next morning our maid was nowhere to be found. I helped myself to some eggs. My brain only had hazy memories of the past night.

Jasper came out, sullen faced, eyes bloodshot red. He blurted instantly, "Did you see it, too?" and without waiting for my affirmation, he moved on to rant about how certain townsfolk are conspiring to rob him of his recently dug treasures and he cannot be separated from his wealth even over his corpse.

He talked about going outside and searching for the burliest man he could find and hiring him to guard the gate, with adequate compensation to wipe out any greed the stranger may possess.

The construction and repairs were slower than usual, on the accounts of no one among the workers having arrived on time. Those who did were drowsy and lethargic, a trait shared by the townsfolk, as the streets were empty until late afternoon.

Having returned after hiring a burly Irishman as a guard, Jasper fetched and cleaned his rifle. Jasper made a plain dinner and we dined silently in a somber mood.

We mutually agreed to stay awake tonight, for whatever

ghoulish foul play was at work might come to a head tonight. He shall not be parted of his wealth, he reiterated before leaving for his chambers while I held back for smoke.

I think I spied him carrying a heavy golden key, which I assumed fits into the corridor's oak doors.

***

It was a beautiful moon, faeries dancing on its silver rays, calling my name. They sang a hauntingly soothing, heartaching song. A wail of longing.

I woke up in my bed, extremely agitated, horrified that I had fallen asleep again. My dreams had betrayed me, playing no doubt, to the moonlit terrors' malicious schemes.

The lack of sleep, hard soil digging, and brainstorming over artifacts had drained the vitality out of me and had injected me with the venom of ghastly terrors of the moon and the drums. As I wiped my sweat and got up from my bed, I heard the familiar sounds again.

The drums! Ethereal, bodiless, sourceless drums from the void.

thump

thump

thump

The cruel assault of terror had begun once more. I had a severe foreboding. Terror filled my heart. I froze in the moment as a fit of dread gripped me, washing my body with a wave of chill.

The night was full moon, and the shadows were stretched beyond imagination. Everything was colored silver white;

shadows were darker and longer. Most fantastic and banished images of blasphemous designs came to my mind.

I controlled my emotions and my body that was giving in to the primitive urges of fear and went to check the three windows, one by one. Despite all of my body trying to negate my will and a deep ingrained sense of fear in my mind warning me not to, I still went ahead.

Alas - I could not have made a bigger mistake. As I toured the windows and peered through them, my dread increased manifold.

Courtyard - empty.

Cliffs - tranquil, shiny, silver sea, soulless.

Street - the horror beyond comprehension!

The warnings of my heart had ultimately proven to be true, and my mind punished me for not paying heed to their incessant noises.

There, on the street I saw a sight to behold.

The entire town was outside.

A humongous procession.

A growing procession.

More and more people came out of houses to join them.

The mobs poured into the streets.

They were dancing.

Dancing in columns of TEN.

Ten again.

Ten steps.

Ten beats.

Ten bodies in every column.

Ten times Ten bodies altogether!!!

The same curious dance of madness; the circles, the turns, the bows and the steps.

The entire procession was dancing but no one made a sound. Only deafening silence. The only noise was that of boots scraping on the cobbled road.

Everyone's head was bowed down, hands clasped behind them. They danced with their feet timed to the beat.
thump
A hundred pairs of feet in unison took a left full turn.
thump
A hundred right feet slid forward.
thump
A hundred people twirled left again in a full circle.
thump
A hundred right feet went forward again.
thump
A hundred heads bowed in obedience.
And the remaining five steps repeated in opposite directions.

It was surreal, almost as if watching one of those moving pictures they currently show in France. They were all bathed in silver moonlight. This allowed me to see clearly what was happening.

I recognized many faces, gaits and physiques even at that distance in the silvery night. They were all sleeping. Same old expressionless faces, eyes shut, cruel smiles on their faces. The procession had everyone. Children, old women, the old man Parker with a limp. All danced, all turned in unison.

Maybe not everyone - as I was watching, mesmerized, hypnotized, and spellbound - I instinctively peeked into our courtyard!
And I saw the burly Irish guard, dancing like a madman,

afflicted with the same fever. I saw him, with much incredulity on my part, join the mob.

I had stepped into the balcony by now, watching this dance of madness.

Anticipating the conclusion, trying to satisfy my primal urge of curiosity, I watched as the procession came up the road to the mansion and disappeared into the forest near the edge of our lawns. I could see no further.

But confusing me was the fact that drums were still beating their fearsome beats.

Do they continue till first light?

Where in the forest do the people go?

Only by sheer bad luck and some grace of the devil did I spy what happened further.

The procession had appeared from the forest and was gathering at the cliff. What followed shook me to my core and left a timeless scar on my soul. It is a subject of much wonder to date of how I still withstood that night, watching the event end.

The mob, now at the cliff, stopped and every ten beats, ten people gathered, took ten steps, and...

Jumped!

I watched in shock and sheer disbelief as I saw the entire town - the demented sleeping faces I once knew - jump - ten by ten after every ten - into the silvery lit sea. The mad dancers, the smiling expressionless faces going into the water off the cliff.

Now inconsolable, and finally free of my hypnotic stare of madness, suicide, drums, and hidden shady desires of my dark heart, I made a dash into my room and packed my belongings. The realization had dawned on me that I was now all alone in an entire town where madness just did a dance of death!

I quickly made a rope out of tied bed sheets and tried to lower myself from the balcony. I did not choose the better path of corridor and stairs for a reason I shall soon reveal in entirety.

Before I could make an attempt, another panicked fear gripped me.

What happened to Jasper?

Surrendering my fear, I reluctantly returned to the room and stepped into the corridor to make for his chamber. But before I could, I was pulled by a mysterious sound. This sound came from closer to my room. Near the thick oak doors in the corridor.

Afraid, I armed myself with a vase and a lamp, and set out to investigate. Moving slowly, panicky, with my heart ready to jump out of my mouth and bid farewell, I made my way.

I quickly discovered the source of sound - a whimpering, a cry, interjected by blabbering of uncertain nature.

The source was a man's shadow, holding a shiny pocket knife-like object, which was sobbing and muttering. Upon closing the distance, my feeble lamp showed - IT WAS JASPER.

The knife in his hand was actually the golden key of those oak doors which he had secretly locked after I had retired late. There was a dark patch on his left eye and blot on his left brow and face. He was lying curled up against those doors.

Now I find it relevant to dutifully explain to my readers that the reason I did not take the obvious path for escape:

I had, on my own conviction, paid the Irishman with hefty remuneration and no small quantities of ale, to bar the doors with a board and nails from outside after we both retired. This was done, for I had worried about myself or my friend wandering off with the hypnotizing beats of the moon.

As I inched closer, I heard him mutter something.

"Are you alright?" I asked him.

To which he mouthed off an utterly otherworldly sequence of words to me. I could not make any sense of it, and to date he has not uttered those words again. I continue to fail in deciphering even a single meaning among those horrid utterances which defy all literature save the ones seen in the translation of those tablets:

"Saw it", "The Cosmic Drum Beater", "Star Spawn", "Ten Headed, Ten Eyed Mad King", "Traveler of Moonlight", "Abode of Moon Faeries", "The One With Ten Faces", "The Listener From The Void", "The Terror Beyond Tongue", "Saw Him, See Him", "Terror of Tens", "The Deity of Ten".

Holding him I now looked at him closely and gasped. For the dark blot was blood. Observing closer, I realized he had gouged out his left eye with the key.

I shook him violently.

"My god man, get it together, what was it?"

"It was the horror... The horror... **THE HORROR TEN TIMES TEN.**"

In the distance, drums...

thump

thump

thump

On The Crevices Of Your Mind

"What are you two looking at?" asked Holly, rolling her eyes.

"Oh… It's nothing too important." replied Alan, as he hastily turned around to face her.

Holly could swear she saw Trish hide something in her pocket. They both looked very startled. Like two thieves caught red handed in the act. Holly found that odd but she ignored it.

"Horror treat anyone? Got this new movie." she asked.

"NO!" came the answer from both, almost before Holly was finished asking.

"You know that exactly isn't my definition of fun." Trish added with disdain.

"Well fine, your loss." Holly waived and walked away.

You see, our Holly wasn't just every other fan who liked horror. Holly lived for them. Lived in them. And when it was just too much, she would ask for more. She spent evenings thinking of such horrors, that a normal person hopes never to dream. She dreamt of terrors and nightmares, and when she ran out of them, she just created more. She watched horror, she drew them and she wrote them.

A Late Night Fright

The feelings, the sudden rush of adrenaline, a wave of chill that rattled the ribs, the rush of goosebumps that swept her whole body. She liked it very much.

She watched horrors until they morphed into her reality. Her thoughts at night played with uncanny shadows, the morning reeked of lonely macabre fantasies. Her winters spent with crackling ambers touching her heart and a horror novel touching her fingertips. She was delighted at the fading sun's play of light. Holly loved the silence of night, with each small sound giving her terrors of the unknown. She looked into darkness, hoping to feel any presence in the dark, that maybe looking at her. The darkness was her chalkboard and she could draw any monster she liked in it.

Today was no different, another invigorating horror film. Holly sat quietly watching it, lights out. As she fell into the world of yet another terror, she felt something. Little uneasiness. The tiny hairs at the back of her neck stood up.
What was it? She turned around and looked. Shadows played in the corner of the room, bathed by light from her television set but this time it was different.

These shadows were little weird, she thought she could make out distinct patterns - the shapes of butterfly, the rose, even a Jason Voorhees mask. Holly thought she was getting too tired. Rest was what she needed, she decided. As she lay down, Holly looked at her wallpaper adorned by classic freaks: Jason, Freddie, Norman, Chucky and others. Normally she would look at them and smile, but today, it was weird. The freaks looked menacing, as if eyeing her, ready to invade her retreat and solitude. Lost in the thoughts, she couldn't tell when she fell into the sweet embrace of sleep.

Next morning, she woke up with a heavy head. 'No work today.' she thought.

"Whoa, you are a mess," Trish said. "You better stay." Trish was a serious, sober girl. She had been dating Alan for quite some time, they worked together. Holly had known Alan since high school. A fact that Trish didn't like much, which Holly assumed was the reason why Trish had been so hostile to Holly ever since Alan introduced the two.

Holly liked the idea of having the day to herself. 'A horror marathon', she smiled wickedly. On a rainy, cloudy day like this? PERFECT! She readied a bowl of cornflakes and started another movie after making herself comfortable on the couch.

As she scooped a mouthful, she felt something. Something moving. Something slimy pressing against her tongue and lips. *MAGGOTS. WORMS.* She immediately spat it out and looked down. Nothing. Just spilt milk and cornflakes. Did she imagine that? 'What? What the hell is happening?' But it was just normal cornflakes. Her rest of day passed uneasy after that.

That night, as she sat watching the TV, something happened again. It began as an itch around her neck, until it grew to a burning sensation. It felt as if someone was strangling her but with a hot rope. She writhed in pain.

"Holly, Holly, wake up! What is wrong with you? Do you need a doctor?" Alan was home in time, only to find Holly screaming on the couch. Holly woke up. It was a dream? But that felt so real.

"I'm fine. I just need some sleep."

Holly didn't understand, it was as if her nightmares were pouring into her reality. The lines seemed to be blurring. They were out to get her. They were hunting her. They wanted her.

She went to bed, only to wake up again in the dead of the night. But this time it was not real. The night and the darkness were not what they were supposed to be. They were plain, almost as if sketched. It looked intense and animated. Almost a pencil art in black and white. Like a picture from a horror book. Was there supposed to be message behind this sight?

Holly felt like she understood. Her horrors were getting to her. They wanted her to join them. They wanted her to be a part of them. Holly suddenly felt peace. It was her dream after all. She got up for a walk, but was unable to. It was as if she was bound, paralyzed. Holly's brain slowly slunk back into the domain of sleep. She woke up to a beautiful sun on her window. So, it was a dream after all. She was disappointed. Her best dream ever - lost. But it was not over yet, was it?

With each passing day her horrors grew, they began taking over her life. Something running out of corner of her eye. Dancing outlines in the shadows. The faces on window glass. Eyes in the cloudy sky spying on her. Creatures from her posters playing hide and seek in her absence.

She skipped work. She skipped calls. All so she could spend a quality time with the terrors her heart created, tricks her mind played. *It was perfect.*

Few days later, one rainy Friday night, Holly finished her dinner early and sat alone on the couch in total darkness, looking out for a horror to occur. ***It did!***

At first it was a scraping of nails on carpet. Like a body dragging itself. She sat in silence peering into darkness. The sound came closer and closer. She could feel her legs ready to give up, breathing got tougher with each passing second. Her heart beat violently in its cage.

And then Holly saw it. It looked like... well it looked like Trish. *What's she doing here?*

"Surprised to see us?" Trish asked.

'Us?' she gasped when Alan walked out too. 'What is the meaning of this?' She tried speaking but her tongue failed to move.

"Sorry hon, we just had to. Nothing personal." Alan smiled.

Holly was losing her breath, her heart slowing down. An excruciating pain shot up her chest. Her mind went numb. Her vision blurred. Her veins bulged out. Alan waved a tiny vial in front of her.

"We gave you your horrors." Alan spoke in a taunting tone. Her vision blurred and eyes slowly closed. Holly's consciousness sunk into the oblivion forever.

Trish put the vial back into her pocket when she felt 'it'. It was piece of paper. She pulled it out. It was a crumpled cutting from an old newspaper that was dated ten years ago. She felt an overwhelming urge to read it then and there.

"Body of Holly Rae, 22 was recovered from her house this morning. Cause of her death was determined to be poisoning in Coroner's preliminary enquiry. A vial recovered at the scene has been sent for further toxicological testing. Her roommate Trish Kirkman, 21 and Alan Matteson, 22, were also found at the scene in a vegetative state. They have been shifted to intensive care. Suspecting foul play, authorities have launched an investigation into the mysterious circumstances the body and roommates were found in."

"What's that?" Alan asked looking at Trish who was trembling by now.

"It says we are in coma." Trish replied.

"That has got to be someone else. Someone with same names."

"Alan, you don't get it do you?"

"What?" asked Alan.

"We killed her. But we didn't finish her story. She is our horror now. She is after us. Her horrors have become ours. Now she lives *on the crevices of our minds...*"

While they were trying to make some sense of things, lights went out. There was a thunder. A blood curdling scream. Shadows and darkness flooded the place like foaming sea wave.

"I am scared, Alan." Trish whispered.

The place became engulfed in darkness and hurricane speed winds poured into the house. But it was over as swiftly as it started and things returned to normal. There was no sign something ever happened in the room. Then they heard approaching footsteps. Someone walked in.

"What are you two looking at?" asked Holly, rolling her eyes.

"Oh… It's nothing too important." replied Alan, as he hastily turned around to face her.

Holly could swear she saw Trish hide something in her pocket. They both looked very startled. Like two thieves caught red handed in the act. Holly found that odd but she ignored it.

"Horror treat anyone? Got this new movie." she asked.

"NO!" came the answer from both, almost before Holly was finished asking.

"You know that exactly isn't my definition of fun." Trish added with disdain.

"Well fine, your loss." Holly waived and walked away.

The Wailer In The Night

"You remember the crossroads behind our apartment, don't you, aunty? The one you can see from our dining room window?" Kaitlynn asked.

"Yes, I do. Why?" Aunt Christa looked at her curiously.

"That's where it all started! Last night I got up for some water and as I walked by the window, I saw it."

"It?" Christa asked.

"It was terrifying. At first, I thought some guy was just carrying a big box on the road. He was moving slow, almost struggling, I would have ignored it if it wasn't 2AM which seemed weird, right?" Kaitlynn explained and her very interested aunt nodded in agreement.

She continued, "It was all very dark, and the man dragged that box slowly, as he scraped it on the gravel. He groaned as if the burden was too heavy to bear. As he neared the crossroads, the light got better and that's when—"

"Here we go again. The drama queen's mega buildup begins." said Sarah, Kaitlynn's younger sister.

"Shut up! I am telling you exactly what I saw! So, this guy enters the well-lit area and aunty, I saw that it wasn't a regular box at all. *It was a coffin*! He was trying to hold one end over his head and just dragged the other end behind him," Kaitlynn added, *"And that's not even the worse part! I saw his face and oh-my-goodness, there was none. His face looked like it had a thick rubbery skin, but stretched so long, it could snap at any moment. Imagine a sheet of skin tightly pulled over a much larger skull. Except his head's shape wasn't human-y either. It was melon-like and depressed in the middle from both sides."*

"That is a great character design. You should be making horror movies!" Christa replied abruptly.

"You aren't listening, aunty!" Kaitlynn said, frustrated "He was dressed in tattered clothes and chains hung from his shoulders. He walked to the center of the crossroads and set his coffin down as his chains rattled. Then he turned towards me!"

"Aw he has a crush on you!" Sarah interrupted once more.

Kaitlynn looked at her angrily, and moved on with her story.

"I don't know how he noticed me, but he turned in my direction, raised that featureless rubber-skin face to look at me. All I saw was a hole instead of a mouth and no eye sockets. And then, he pointed at me and immediately came a loud bellowing. I swear, I was so badly scared. It started as a low whistle that turned into a constant moan, that grew and grew into loud wailing and didn't stop. I closed the window and ran back to the bed and buried myself in the pillow. I could still hear him until I grew too tired and fell asleep."

"Whoa, that's some nice imagination! I admit I got goosebumps. Great story." Christa grinned.

Christa tried to recreate the scene in her head. She remembered the place clearly, having been to the apartments many times. The third-floor window gave a direct view to the empty field behind Kaitlynn's apartments. Cutting through the field was the country crossroads. The field was pretty barren and there were not many trees or buildings nearby. In one corner of the gravel crossroads existed a solitary pole with a yellow sodium street light. There were no other signs or traffic lights. She would see a few vehicles pass by from time to time but traffic was usually low on these rural roads.

She thought about the man with thick rubbery skin, standing under yellow light in the dead of the night, looking at her with an eyeless face. The light bathed his figure as he stood in the center blocking her path. Wailing loudly with increasing intensity as he pointed towards her. The thought alone gave her chills.

"Scared you, didn't I? Careful, the wailer might visit you tonight!" Kaitlynn's laughter boomed, while she tried acting like a hunched zombie, attempting to imitate the wailer.

"Fine, you win tonight. Next time we have a game night, be ready to lose. Where did you even come up with such a strange idea?" Christa enquired.

"Her Highness goes to bed late, dreams weird stuff and then wakes up late." Sarah poked in again.

"Oh, I thought it really did happen, but then I don't remember waking up for water or anything. I asked Sarah and also our neighbors, the Weavers. No one heard anything. Impossible. The way he screamed he would have woken up two blocks. Bad dream, that is all. Worked for me, as my story time was the best tonight." Kaitlynn smirked.

"No, that would be mine." Sarah demanded.

"You really need to start sleeping early and stop thinking about monsters. Two words: NOT REAL." Christa advised Kaitlynn and she was serious.

"Yeah, I will try, aunty." Kaitlynn's demeanor changed momentarily as she looked down and bit her lips.

Christa spied Kaitlynn's expression change to one of sadness and felt like she was being secretive. But immediately it returned to normal.

"Monsters are real. Look at this one here." Kaitlynn replied as she gently tapped Sarah's forehead. Both sisters started to argue again.

Christa laughed and prepared to drop them off to their apartment. The sisters never got along in front of others, but under the surface they were nearly inseparable. These girls had seen so much rotten luck very early in life, losing their dad first and later their mother. They were temporarily under Christa's care, their only remaining relative, but they had moved out to their own apartment as soon as they were adults.

Kaitlynn was 19 but waited for Sarah to turn 18 before moving away with her. One year had passed since they left to build their own life. Christa fully supported them being independent but she was always worried. Kaitlynn could handle herself, but Sarah's gift of sight was taken away by a disease at a very young age. She compensated that by being bold and bratty. It worked mostly but Sarah was still a little child at heart and needed her older sister to protect her from the world. And Christa would protect them both.

***

A somber mood hung over Christa's house and people talked in hushed voices while standing in small groups. Occasionally someone would sob or cry. People hugged each other, offered condolences or stood alone aimlessly. The air was heavy with grief. There was not much attendance beyond friends or workmates. All the relatives that attended, belonged to Christa's side of the family and hardly any of them knew Kaitlynn.

Sarah sat quietly in one corner, totally disheveled. Her blue eyes may look lifeless, but puffy skin and a trail of dried tears told their own tale. She didn't talk to anyone and only nodded politely if anyone talked to her. Christa made sure to check on her every few minutes.

The loss was not only irreplaceable but also unhealable. Sarah had lost her anchor, her best friend and only family left. Christa not only had to grieve for Kaitlynn but also make sure Sarah somehow returned to the world. She had to care for Sarah's well-being and give her all the support she needed.

Kaitlynn left them suddenly a few days ago. Sarah was the one who found her, accidentally running into her lifeless body on the floor, early in the morning when she went to wake Kaitlynn up. Nothing suspicious was found, except her heart had just naturally stopped. No one knew why and no explanations were ever offered. It had barely been a month since that game night, the last time they were all together.

Christa tried her best to persuade Sarah to move back in with her but was respectfully turned down.

"I will be fine, aunt Christa. I know the apartment layout very well and Jess comes twice a day to help me with the cleaning and dishes. The nurse also drops by daily to check on me. Do you want me to baby proof the apartment too?"

"I know but all I want is the best for—" Christa pleaded again.

Sarah was exasperated by the constant nudging. "I need to learn to live by myself. No one is going to be there forever to look after me. And guess who I will call first if I ever need any help?"

Christa had to relent to her stubborn niece. There was no winning this fight. She dropped Sarah off at her apartment. Afterwards, she swore to herself to look out for her. She tried to visit Sarah almost daily, and assisted her with her finances and suitable work. Few weeks passed by, and while it was tough for both, they overcame their challenges. For a moment, everything looked good, almost normal even.

***

One crisp afternoon, as Christa sat watching her TV, her door flew open and without a warning, a very distraught Sarah barged in. She was wildly shivering and very panicky. Her very concerned aunt rushed to her aid, helping her settle down as she tried to figure out what made her niece so agitated.

After some coffee, Sarah settled down into quiet sobs before Christa dared to ask her what had transpired. Sarah never lifted her face up as she recounted her story.

"There is something you don't know, aunty. Weeks before *that* day Kaitlynn was getting more and more paranoid. She was losing sleep. Twice she told me stories about that… thing… that she saw. She saw him again at night a few more times. She heard his wailing." Sarah spoke softly.

She elaborated further, "Of course, I never believed her. I never heard any of it. Neither did the neighbors or anyone in the building. I know that because Kaitlynn asked everybody."

"Why didn't either of you girls tell me anything?" Christa asked, looking concerned.

"We didn't believe it, even Kaitlynn didn't. And what can I see? Nothing at all. There was no proof any of it was real, that it wasn't just a story, until…"

"Until?"

"Until last night… I was lying in my bed but didn't feel sleepy at all. Suddenly, I heard it – as clear as day – a faint whistling like a kettle. It came from far away. My body froze, and I am not exaggerating. I felt numb. I just lay silently as the whistling turned into a moan and kept increasing in intensity. It was an unbroken, consistent wailing that kept getting louder. On top of it I also heard the clanking of chains."

"What did you do, then?" Christa asked.

"Do? I tried moving until my body actually responded, then I felt my way to the door and quickly ran to knock at the neighbor's door. The Weavers were very nice to me and they let me stay the night. The sounds stopped when I was in their apartment. And guess what? They heard no wailing. Mr. Weaver himself drove me over here."

"You are not going back there. Live with me, there is plenty of room. This has always been your home and you are always welcome; you know that."

Sarah grew quiet. She was contemplating yet another life-changing decision she was about to make. This place was safe, she wouldn't be alone. Aunt Christa will look after her and there was no shame in asking family for help.

"Aunty, I think I will move back. I am scared of what will happen if I don't. It seems stupid, this wailer and stuff… but after Kaitlynn… It was so real. She was right all this time. I wish

I had listened to her earlier."

Feeling relieved, Christa reassured her. "It's not your fault. Don't blame yourself for anything. You did the right thing."

Christa had a hard time believing the events that Sarah narrated. She was too logical. Yet somehow, she felt the fear deep within her heart. It could have been a bad dream, a nightmare, no doubt inspired by Kaitlynn's stories and molded by Sarah's grief. Still, the poor girl was terrified and shivering in fear. She wouldn't just abandon someone she raised as her own child. She convinced Sarah to wait and relax, as she went back to the apartments to pack her belongings.

The clock was already pointing towards 10 P.M. by the time Christa was finished packing and labeling contents from barely two rooms. She would just have to come back the next day to finish the rest. The packing was hectic and disorganized but everything that happened in the apartment so far was uneventful. A sense of uneasiness lay heavy on her mind.

Christa was swiftly filling, taping and arranging the boxes in the dead silence of the night. Only sounds breaking the eerie silence were the scissors, tape and bubble wrap. All went fine until suddenly her ears perked up. She thought she could hear a peculiar sound. It was very faint, so she listened intently, dropping the tasks at hand. And sure enough, hiding behind the clock's tic and toc in the silent night, was a faint whistling sound!

***

Back at the house, Sarah suddenly woke up, feeling uncomfortable and called out for her aunt. Hearing no response, she got up, grabbed her walking stick and went to look for her aunt. Aunt Christa wasn't home yet and the door was locked. '10 P.M.' her phone's voice-clock declared. She assumed her aunt would be returning soon. She felt famished, and being familiar with the layout of the house, made her way to the fridge.

Sarah stretched her arm out to the expected position of the fridge handle… *and recoiled it in terror!*
As her hand moved forward, it hit an obstruction. The barrier felt soft, rubbery and large and it stood straight in front of her and the fridge. Her heart started pounding as the sudden shock and fright engulfed her. She stood there frozen in terror, not knowing what to do.

After a brief moment, she gathered the courage and gently extended her hand in the expected direction of the barrier again. Nothing. Just the cold surface of the fridge. She tried listening but could not hear anyone or anything moving. Not hungry anymore, she decided to call her aunt first.

She was just about to give a voice command for a call, when she heard a whistling. Sarah was familiar with the tune and knew what it meant. Panicking, Sarah moved back and tripped over the furniture. And in doing so she dropped her phone. She frantically looked for it. By now, the whistling had grown into a wailing and sounded much louder as it echoed across the kitchen.

Finding the phone under the kitchen counter with her fingertips, she quickly activated the voice command feature, only for the phone to pick up the wailing over her voice and fail to identify her voice commands. The constantly booming wail now shook up the house and rattled the glass.

Loud wailing echoed on the walls and reverberated through

the house. Chains clanked in the background. The sound kept coming closer towards her. Sarah thought that the only logical option left would be to crawl to her room nearby, lock the door, bury herself into the beddings and try to use her phone again in a hopefully much calmer environment.

Sarah made a successful escape into her room and locked it. She slid under the mattress of her bed (as the sheets provided no respite), which temporarily muffled the unearthly noises. She pulled out her phone to give it a voice command to make a call to aunt. At that very moment, her door flew open.

Sarah wasn't able to witness the very tall man or the creature that now stood in the doorway. He was dressed in a tattered old Victorian era tailcoat, with chains wrapped around its neck and shoulders. On the floor behind him lay an old coffin. The thing raised and pointed a finger at Sarah. Finally, its deformed, rubbery face let out a high-pitched wail through the gaping hole in its featureless, eyeless face.

Sarah covered her ears due to pain. Her head was splitting apart making her dizzy. Everything turned dark around her.

***

Christa tried to search for the source of the unearthly whistling. She followed it to the dining room, where the window was open. She peered outside and squinted her eyes. The scenery was quite familiar to her even at night. Yet, there was an unexpected sight tonight, that was neither familiar nor welcome.

Christa watched as a man walked slowly on one of the roads passing the crossroads. He was slowly dragging something behind him. She gasped as the light from the lone bulb immersed him in brightness and she saw him clearly for the first time. He met the exact mental image she had formed of him from Kaitlynn's story. 'Kaitlynn was right.' She thought, 'Every word. She kept this horror to herself because I didn't believe her.'

Soon another new wave of horror washed over her before guilt could set in. The man or rather a monster, as he reached to the center of the crossroads, stopped and put down his burden. Then he turned to face her, raised his head, pointed at her and wailed with intensity increasing quickly. This jolted Christa back into reality and she noticed more things about the scene. At the man's feet lay his coffin, but things were different, as it was open and occupied. Even in the dull yellow light, the darkness and the distance, it was unmistakable. The same dress, the dark glasses, the same hairstyle. *In the coffin lay Sarah.*

Horrified, Christa instinctively rushed towards the door. She did not have a plan or the time to think of one. Only to stop dead in her tracks when she heard some commotion coming from Kaitlynn's locked bedroom that lay ahead to the left of her path. It sounded like a shuffle, followed by a groan. Soon came the sound of a box being dragged. A sound that clearly gave all indications of what was to follow. Christa ran faster, running by the bedroom door and unlocked the front door.

The last thing Christa saw as she shut her door was Kaitlynn's door opening and an outline of a tall figure standing in the darkness as it let out a groan. She locked the door and turned to face the corridor. The corridor was uncharacteristically dark tonight and all the lights in there seemed dim. Without wasting any time, she instantly ran and banged on the neighbor's doors but no response came. Her screams or the loud moaning of the creature didn't seem to have affected the Weavers at all.

The sounds of groans and heavy footsteps in Sarah's apartments were growing closer. Deciding on a newer course of action, Christa went for the elevator and pressed the button. The elevator started climbing up slowly. There was not enough time left as the apartment doorknob was rattling with force.

'Stairs!' Her brain yelled. With a mad dash Christa reached the staircase at the far end of the corridor and pulled out her phone to use its flashlight. She didn't turn around to witness that her door was open now and there stood a tall, skinny figure, silently watching her run away.

Using the flashlight, she started quickly jumping down the stairs, skipping a few steps at a time. Christa had barely gone down one floor when she heard the clanking of chains coming from below. Yet again, she had to stop to monitor the path ahead. Looking down into the darkness, Christa held her phone with her hand stretched out over the railings. The tiny flashlight feebly lighting the empty chasm below. The chains rattled again, breaching the absolute silence.

Watching intently, she scanned the stairway of the level directly below her. Slowly a figure's head poked out over the railing. It was the wailer, just on the floor beneath her! He turned his head towards her and looked directly at her. This was the first time Christa got to witness the wailer closely. Every freaky detail was exactly as Kaitlynn had described. The rotten, rubbery green skin on the bulbous deformed and featureless head, the chains around his shoulders and his tattered tailcoat.

Christa screamed at the grotesque sight and turned around

to run. Within a few seconds she was back to where she had started, panting loudly. There was no question of going back into the apartment and the neighbors still hadn't answered the door. She prayed while running to the elevator and luckily found it waiting, thanks to her earlier call. She walked in and pressed the basement floor button.

Every moment felt like a million years as the door shut. In that final moment, and unannounced, the wailer's arm lunged at her from the dark corridor. She shrieked in shock. However, the only thing that happened was the wailer's nails scratching the metal surface in an unsettlingly loud manner.

3… 2… 1… As the floors counted down, her panic increased. The wailer had seemingly appeared from the crossroads to the apartment and from behind her to the floor below her. Now that he was left somewhere above, how long will it take for him to reappear down below? What if he is already waiting there? The elevator reached the basement and the door slid open… and nothing jumped out.

Ignoring the utter darkness in the basement, Christa made a beeline for her car. She was shaking in fear and was trying to avoid looking at anything else. At that point, her only plan was getting out of there alive and how to rescue Sarah hadn't even started to register in this new list of priorities. Sarah was in the coffin but Christa couldn't even generate the courage to boldly face him.

Christa got into the car and buckled herself, right as the relentless pursuer reappeared. The wailer, tied down by his burden, was always slow, even though he never stopped chasing his victims until they eventually ran right into him. She hit the gas and off she went, leaving the monster standing. A low guttural growl shook the basement.

***

The car sped on the pothole filled road as Christa calmed her nerves. Cold night wind washed her face and kept her vigilant. Millions of thoughts shot through her mind. Fighting with that monstrosity was not on the cards. Accessing the coffin unnoticed was impossible as it was always on his back. Police will never believe her and the Weavers had slept through the commotion. Priests? Religion?

Lost in her thoughts, she didn't notice how far or how long she had traveled on the dark country road before her attention returned to the road. Looking up ahead, she spotted a faintly lit-up area. It was a ray of hope in the completely dark countryside. But as she got closer, the speed decreased until the car came to a complete stop.

Christa gasped audibly, as she found herself staring at those very crossroads in front of her that she had always seen from Kaitlynn's apartment many times before. But now the place felt menacing. A sinister aura hung at the place at night.

She didn't even realize when she turned towards the crossroads in an entirely opposite direction. 'This is not possible.' Christa thought, 'I drove straight towards home, not going around the apartment complex.' She tried processing her situation but was too baffled to recall anything.

Clank. The ringing metallic sound drew her attention. *Clank. Skraaashhh.* Again. The wailer appeared, dragging the coffin behind him, his chains making a racket with each movement. He groaned in pain as he dragged the heavy burden with a lot of

47

effort on his arched back. She watched as he walked into the center of the crossroads and was bathed in the light from her car's headlights. Then, in an action very familiar, he looked at Christa, pointed to her and wailed.

It was a time for fight or flight, and Christa's heart decided to fight. That decision was the first moment of clarity she had ever since the monster started pursuing her tonight. Slowly her foot pressed into the accelerator and her grip tightened. The car started rolling swiftly towards the target, rapidly building momentum. She was determined now and the distance was adequate for her car to gain enough speed.

Her car rammed into the target with a heavy thud and a heavy mist engulfed the scene as the wailer melted into nothingness. Christa controlled her car as it swerved in the road, bringing it to a halt. She looked back. Nothing. Christa then leaned out of the window cautiously. Just a dissipating mist. Then what was it that had left a massive dent in her car? What created that noise?

Christa got out and walked back to the spot. The mist was nearly gone and a mangled clump of mass lay in the center of the crossroads, showered in yellow light. Her eyes bulged with the realization and a heart wrenching scream pierced the veil of night. She had just killed Sarah…

***

The proceedings were swift, and the sentencing was swifter. Christa didn't put up any fight. Secretly, everyone was grateful for that. Every single little detail was played out in the media. Yet, no one could establish any motive and so, people created their own theories. Evidence all pointed to Christa but no one in the entire apartment complex ever heard anything. Among all of it, the only thing Christa did was either cry or remain quiet and accept all that happened. Deep inside, the safety of jail, cameras and crowd offered her a hope, a sense of security from the wailer.

'The wailer walked slowly, dragging his coffin behind him. Christa knew this time it was for her. He groaned as he dragged his burden in the corridor, the chains rattling against the bars. His nails dug into the coffin he held on his back. He arrived and stood in front of her cell which was lit up by a dull flickering light. No one in the adjoining cells seemed to notice him. The wailer looked at Christa with his decaying rubbery soulless face, and pointing to her, he wailed. It started as a low whistle but kept on increasing continuously in intensity until it became unbearable... aaaaaaaaaaAAAAAAAA....'

"AAAAAAAHHHH" Christa woke up screaming. The noise also woke up everyone else in nearby cells and a prison guard came running to check the commotion. Christa looked around and took a deep breath. She knew what was going to be her fate. He is waiting. He is hungry. He is patient but he will get her. Eventually. He always gets his victims. The empty coffin awaits...

The Guest That Midnight Called

She thought she heard something, but nothing was there. Just emptiness, a void in the dark, darker than the secrets she held. She thought she saw something, but when she looked again, nothing. Her fears slowly crept into her heart, invading her surety and strengthening her doubts.

She felt like she was being followed, she scanned the area and saw nothing. Was she being watched? No eyes were on her, at least none she could detect. Did something just brush her arm? She looked around but all she could find were her own shadows.

So, she kept walking. But no matter where she went, she couldn't shake the feeling that she wasn't alone. By now, she had reached the stairs. She tried peeking downstairs from the landing.

Her mind was in a state of absolute frenzy. A sense of dread, primeval fears, horror of unknown and a terror of darkness assaulted her mind.

Her heart was a different story altogether. It was beating a fast tune, a symphony of dread, a ballad of adrenaline playing through her veins.

thump

thump thump

thump thump

thump thump

Her poor heart couldn't decide whether to continue playing that wretched orchestra or cease its ruckus forever.

She decided to go downstairs and see what lurker haunts her house and her dreams tonight. She crept cautiously, taking one step at a time, ensuring no sound came from her feet. As soon as she reached the bottom step, the clock struck twelve in the midnight and the bells chimed in loudly with a menacing echo!

The violent shock of such a sudden noise rattled her bones and shook her nerves. One can only assume how much effort the heart would have had to spend in continuing the onerous task of pumping the blood. She grabbed her aching chest and leaned back against the wall, gasping for a breath.

She was covered in sweat now, strands of her red hair clung to her brow as sweat drops glistened in the pale moonlight that filtered through her window. She took a deep breath to compose herself and started moving again, walking down the corridor as softly as a butterfly.

The floor was cold against her bare feet, the wooden boards hugged them like a mad hopeless romantic separated from his muse. She felt a draft coming from somewhere, like someone had opened a window. It was a simple stream, a zephyr, a kiss of nature on her neck.

The hair on the back of her neck stood up with goosebumps and a frightful wave of chill raced down her spine. She looked down the corridor and back to the stairs.

Darkness. A black void.

Eerie, unfathomable darkness.

Blinding, soothing, calming and yet unnerving.

Too far to go back now, she must go ahead. Ahead, to look for the visitor. The visitor of the night.

What was it that this sunless sky had cooked up from the deepest pits of all that is unholy?

Who was the visitor in the shadow, one who she must now find?

Who did the wretched night invite to her house?

What hateful thing was it that destroyed her sleep, her peace and filled her soul with terror?

Who was it? This guest? The guest that midnight called?

It was well past the gloomy midnight now; she didn't know where her feet were taking her. Like a lost soul attracted to wisp o' the will, she drifted ahead.

The night was getting colder, the kind of cold that seeped into your bones chilling you to your core and freeze your soul, but still she walked onward till she found the kitchen, unperturbed by the changed surroundings.

In the morning it was usually filled with the smell of coffee and damp boards. Visuals of moldy, bloated wood panels, unkempt dishes, disused equipment and nearly rotten food always greeted her in the day.

But now it was bathed completely in dark, with darkness secretly dancing their mad dance all around in the moonlight that sneaked in through the window. The sheer dauntlessness of their naked wild dance on moonlit boards, while she herself was abjectly terrified, were an insult to her senses. A mockery of her terror and a welcome for her shadowy guest.

She imagined the shadows take fantastic shapes in the cover

of darkness. She would be none the wiser if they were making fun of her fears. She would be clueless if they hid the intruder amongst themselves, too.

The kitchen was silent, waiting, watching, anticipating.

The absolute terror of darkness and unknown lulled the unusual creakiness of old wooden boards into stillness and silence. She felt around for the little cabinet and succeeded! She could no longer depend on the moonlight, her only ally in darkness. So, she pulled out a little flashlight from the cabinet. It flickered and almost gave out, for the ages of neglected meted to its batteries by its owner had taken its toll.

Armed with a much better but slightly unreliable source of light, she surged ahead. A warm feeling gushed through her, no doubt a reassured heart working double time. Such is the power of a little luminescence and adrenaline. Cautiously and 'excitedly', she surged ahead, with terror slowly giving way to a momentary speck of curiosity and bravery.

The weak beam showered the kitchen one corner at a time, drenching everything in a yellow beam, creating unfathomable images as the light interweaved with the shadows, temporarily dissolving the darkness in very small areas. She walked, meticulously covering the corners, the shelves and cupboards.

Nothing. Not even a mouse. The shadows melted like butter meeting a hot knife wherever the flashlight pointed.
Still nothing.

She had completed a meticulous search of the entire house. All corners were probed, all closets checked, all doors locked behind her.
Is the visitor of night gone?
Her unexpected curse, the uninvited guest of midnight…

Gone?

NO! it didn't feel so. The dread stayed in her heart. She still didn't feel safe. She must look once more. She must confront the terror and her fears once again.

At that very instance, she heard it.

Rustling.

Muffled sound of walking.

Corridor?

It felt like an invitation. She dreaded it. It could be a challenge, a taunt, a ridicule, an…an ambush?

But she must go, she must look. She needed her answers. Needed the clarity. With this thought of eventuality, lack of options and abundance of finality, she trudged towards the corridor. That's when her flashlight breathed its last and abandoned her.

Comic fate or cruelty? Curse of Greek goddess Hecate? A cruel play of the sisters of fate? Why now? She could not believe her fortunes. Resigned and defeated, she adapted moonlight and luck as her allies once more.

As she walked through dark corridor, the sounds were getting louder, but those were only her breathing and her heartbeats, reaching the deafening pitch once more.

She was getting very close now. Immediately, a sudden wave of claustrophobia hit her, as if the walls were suddenly moving in to capture her in their ever-tightening embrace. For a moment she felt feverish and nauseated, felt the breath get hot, putrid and smelling like acid. Like she was about to empty her stomach due to intense attack of the dread.

She finally regained the control of her senses with extreme willpower and swung around reflexively.

A draft of wind brushed her. A song called her. She could not explain it. The calming song had a hypnotizing effect on her. Her feet turned towards the source of the tune, no longer led by her brain.

She walked towards the door. The door was ajar…

By now, she was beyond the realm of fear and curiosity. No morbid thoughts worried her anymore. She floated towards the door, half asleep and trance-like, as if pulled by a magnet. It was the song, a faint whistle, mixed with buzz of crickets, wind piping and subtle sounds of her house, that controlled her like a puppet.

She opened the door and stepped onto the porch.

And there he was.

Her guest.

Her uninvited guest.

There, in the corn field.

Showered in pale moonlight.

Oh! The horror, her celestial ally made her guest look even more menacing now.

He stood there silently, facing away from her.

Faint streams of mist ran around him.

Covering him, then exposing him, like in a game of hide and seek.

Gentle breeze washed her, bringing her terror to the fore once more. Corns meanwhile gently swayed with the breeze, uncaring and free. Dancing their own dance, bowing side to side with the wind. She looked at him for the longest time but he never turned. By ignoring her completely, he was making her quest for him meaningless.

It was all too painfully quiet. It felt like the time had paused.

She prayed he would do something.
She prayed she would do something.
He didn't move, her feet froze.
If there is anything worse than running into a terror, it is facing the terror till eternity.

Her mind registered everything. Every feeling, every sensation, every thought and fear.
It counted her heart beats.
Every touch of the cold breeze on her skirt.
The timed swaying of corn stalks.
The misty curtain between her and her visitor.
A branch of tree hitting the side of the house somewhere.
flap
thock
flap

What will happen?
Climax reached its peak.
Her guest nodded while looking away,
and vanished...
And that was it.
An underwhelming conclusion to her night of terrors.

She was dazed by her trials of midnight.
A random visitor, a random reason.
And for what? Why was he here?
Why the game of cat and mouse?

She solemnly got back in and secured her door latch. She was sleepy now, with terror giving way to tiredness. With floating feet, she came up the stairs.
Back to her bedroom.
Back to her castle of dreams.

Back where.... *It all had started.*

Where the unnamed shadow, the guest of midnight had first greeted her.

She stood there at the door, clutching the knob reluctantly. Trying to drum up some support from within, reassuring herself her tribulations were over. That there was nothing to fear, no cause of dread.

Night of horrors - over!

Overcoming the dread again, she walked in and took few steps forward.

That's when she noticed something she hadn't seen before.

A shadow on the ground.

A crumpled object on the floor.

A shriveled thing in the dark.

The object was a lifeless body, its outline became visible as her eyes adjusted to the darkness better.

It was the body of a young red-haired woman.

Caressed by sharp beams of moonlight. Hand outstretched. Crimson pearls of blood covered it.

The body was cold. Unattended. Sad. Broken.

She was confused, yet her memories returned slowly. They had their fun but it was time to remember now. It all started coming back to her.

The knife.

The warm feeling of blade in her wrist.

Creeping coldness that crept as her soul left her body. Cloudiness that surrounded her as she closed the eyes.

It was all clear now.

Breaking her chain of thoughts, there came a sudden knock from the window. She turned around, unafraid and incurious.

It was a shadow at the window and it was blocking the moonlight from coming into the room.

Her guest!!! He was back again.

"Come, child."

She paused for a moment. Looking at her lifeless body, elegant, a piece of art.

She thought about her empty house, her youth, her memories, a lost love, no family. This life had given her nothing. And there was nothing left to stay behind for. No one to stay behind for. She made up her mind quickly and smiled with relief. A lone tear fell down her cheek.

She turned around to face the shadow which was now inside the room, held its hand tightly and *left forever with the guest of midnight, her guide from beyond.*

Cheyenne

The people looked around nervously.
The carnival was dark and gloomy.
Smooth cold wind whispered one word…
"Cheyenne"….
Silent parents stood together with their quiet kids.
Shopkeepers waited without light in their eyes.
In the absence of any sound from the crowd, even the tiniest noise reigned supreme.
The crunch of sugar candies.
The crackling embers in the fire pit.
Parents knew it was a mistake.
Thinking carnival would lift their mood, after all that had happened in their little town.
"Cheyenne"….
The name that came to mind with every cold breeze.
She had left an impact on town. She did.
The name she etched on the park bench.
Her locker at the school, still full of her belongings.
The tree under whose shade her car was always seen parked.
The empty lot where she was found…
What happened that unfortunate year when the children…

NO!

Some stories are better left unfinished.

The story like that of…

***"Cheyenne"* ….**

The parents didn't want to talk about it. Or the police. Or bus drivers.

Not her classmates. Not even the teachers.

But what was it, that sent the chills down the spine tonight? Everyone had their eyes to the cloudy sky tonight after a good day of rain.

It was cold, windy and the carnival was dead.

***"Cheyenne"* ….**

A gust of wind said.

It was time to leave.

The carnival idea clearly didn't work. To home then.

It was a crowd.

But it didn't feel safe.

People walked silently in twos and threes. Some had cars.

Gloomy children, who didn't seem even slightly excited at winning cuddly toys or holding ice cream cones, walked sadly alongside.

They looked like caricatures of humankind. Walking silently on streets, dark paths, wet and cold from the rain. Sending shadows on walls, a pit pat of wet shoes echoed.

***"Cheyenne"* ….**

Unnerving gusts of wind, made their wet bodies miserable.

Tonight, just a cat going through trash in an alleyway made more sound than this crowd.

Even the accursed silence would be louder tonight.

But what exactly was the dread that hung in the air tonight, no one could point at.

Dim streetlamps flickered and wind that blew away paper and jacket flaps alike, making the people wrap them tighter around their bodies, their last safe refuge against the chill in their bones.

*Almost as if **"Cheyenne"** put her hand gently on your shoulder.*

Is that thought, the real reason for shivers down their spines? A gust of wind flew by again, damp, cold and carrying the unfathomable, unbearable fear.

"Cheyenne" ….

There is this family we don't know anything about.

They, like everyone else thought the carnival would be great for their mood and town.

It wasn't to be.

They hurried home. Walking fast. Not stopping for anything.

Their kid, in a semi state of being dragged and running.

There was no traffic to worry about anyway.

Just dark dead empty streets with puddles that reflected yellow lamps.

Shadows circled around them.

The shadows seemed to unite into the most unnatural and surreal forms that can only be dreamt up by the darkest corners of the human mind.

The horror, the curiosity, indescribable, unearthly, that puts the deepest dreams of writers and mad romantics to shame.

Did the shadow follow them?

Do winds know where they are?

"Cheyenne"….

The name that a flurry of air whistled to them.

What insane fear lurks today in these streets? The family neared home, safe and away from shadows, and then…

A Scream.

A blood curdling scream, and *then three more!*

A paralyzing wave of numbing terror made them immobile. Their faces were flushed with horror.

Their hearts took the worst, almost ready to cease working.

Was it from a street before the crossroads they just ran past? Didn't it contain another few families?

Hurrying past, huddled into silent groups, reassuring their children and heads bowed down, as if to avoid any infernal terror, that perchance may present itself from an unexpected corner of this concrete jungle.

What now? Nothing can be done!

Their pace quickened and a few more puddles splashed higher under the press of their boots.

So near, the thought about distance, both of the house ahead and a lurking horror behind, renewed them with vigor.

Wind blew again, touching them, caressing the hair like a lover that adores your presence in their lap.

The name rose in the sky, the hateful, fearsome, terrifying name,

"Cheyenne"....

They had to make it, and make it they did.

Wind hit them with a gentle smirk as they entered and shut the door behind.

And that was that, the terror that claimed people, and may still be trying, for any poor soul unlucky enough to be caught outside.

Relieved, they rushed to change and head to bed, for what was there to do anymore?

Have the frenzied assaults of chill on their damp clothes not been enough?

They retreated together and tucked their child in-between, before settling into the bed silently.

Praying the night comes to pass, and the horror does not last.

They hoped the cost wouldn't be too high, or the nightmare wouldn't extend into eternity.

The town has paid enough. It has suffered enough.

These thoughts and savageries of the day had been too much for them, soon their eyes drifted into the arms of sleep.

Sweet embrace of soothing dreams overcame them, and a fleeting stream of chilly wind swept over them.

Wind?

The woman, half floating in the realm of slumber, asked, "Do we have a window open?"

The husband woke up in a fit of horror.

The name called for them,

"Cheyenne" ....

Next day the townsfolk took a count of their losses.

Grief was covering every face, solemn and silent.

As the day progressed, people took stock of situation, calling and meeting.

Someone drove down to this family's house.

The lone house was tranquil and silent, uncaring of previous nights' bad dreams.

There they were greeted by a single word, etched into the door.

It was a name, in a teen girl's handwriting, well-practiced beautiful copperplate cursive.

A signature that was all too familiar to townspeople.

"Cheyenne" ....

Cat Among The Pigeons

I lay in my bed quietly, looking at the ceiling. In the dark night there was nothing but a void to look at. I turned my head towards the open door, my bed strategically aligned to give me a full view of the hallway and the stair landing. To my dismay, the darkness had swallowed them whole too. I tried hearing for any noise but save for some critters, nothing extraordinary broke the silence. Even as my much-alarmed brain urged me to decide my next course of action, my tired body just refused to budge. I was aware my continued inaction will eventually allow the predator to reach its prey. **Me.**

I kept straining my eyes into the pitch-black world outside the room, trying to recall a mental image of doors, railings and stairs. No power, no light source and no moon, natural light was not an ally tonight. My thought momentarily drifted towards the empty rooms downstairs. Who and what madness was lurking there in solitude? I shivered at the thought of someone or something, patiently waiting below.

Recovering my chain of thoughts, I looked out again. This time something had changed. What I saw may be slightly unexplainable on my part, but to my best attempt, I saw a slightly darker mass forming by the top stair, slowly but steadily, in the absolute darkness of night. Either my eyes had adapted slightly better to the darkness during the preceding few moments or my tired eyes were playing tricks on me. The darker mass grew larger against the backdrop of the tenebrous dark nature of the night, distinctly appearing like it was crawling closer.

At that moment I got up, walked to the door and after peering into the absolute nothingness, I slammed the door shut and latched it! That meant my survival instincts were still kicking because the action was wholly unplanned and way more energetic than anticipated. Having accomplished that, I slumped down on my bed again.

I shut my eyes, focusing only on sounds. Soon enough, faint muffled sounds came from outside the door. There was a slight creak, as the locked door groaned from being gently pushed inwards. Then came another sound, the very gentle squeaking of the doorknob being turned. After two very gentle clicks and a tap, the knob returned into its place. Another soft thud echoed in the silence, indicating a final forceful attempt was being made and then the sound of careful and muffled footsteps going down the hallway; a sign of surrender.

"Damn right, not today." I smirked to myself as the attempts to open my door ceased. "You will not take me today."

***

Moving to a new place had always been easy for me. My belongings were scarce and so were my attachments. So, when the opportunity to research the deepest lores of New England knocked, there was nothing that could hold me back. Within days of receiving an initial offer from an acquaintance, I had already reached my destination.

The quaint little town of Helmsbury had only 3000 residents. The town held no significance to any unassuming traveler, but to those of us who knew, its ancient William C. Sullivan library, named after its founder, held the rarest books dealing with mysticism and witchcraft. The library itself was tiny and much of its content came from the founder's personal writings and collections. All such content was kept under strict secrecy from common society, save for those truly interested and those who were in the trade, leaving very little reason for the townsfolk to look for them. A much newer section with recent books of all genres was later added to attract the youth and the older section slowly exited the public memory.

The town had seen some semblance of modernity with new roads and power, but at its heart, it was still a settlement pincered by dense primeval forests and enveloped by ancient myths that had traveled down the generations by word of mouth. I noted, after spending several days of touring and socializing, that the townsfolk avoided the green woods with fear and sometimes, reverence. None dared venture too deep and wood logging was shallow. Even farmlands and pastures stayed clear of the forest borders. There seemed to be a certain unspoken understanding among the people and everyone brushed aside my queries about the forest nonchalantly.

My primary concern on moving was lodging but that was immediately resolved when I rented the colonial era house on the Cavendish Hill. The house was not very dilapidated despite lack of maintenance and had power, but it was entirely too large for just one dweller. It was located on a small hillock named after an explorer and overlooked the entire town. The distance from the nearest cottage was significant and the pine and oak trees surrounded the house from three sides. A lone road snaked its path under a tunnel formed by tree canopy, rising abruptly on the steep terrain to reach the house. This however, was a gift to my lonesome self, the house providing the necessary peace and solitude I needed for my research. I set up my desk and chair facing the study room's tall window that displayed the town skyline and the sea of trees that wrapped the town from two sides, divided by the new highway.

After giving myself a few days to settle in and explore the town while trying to make some local connections, I set up to fulfill my originally planned mission. My good friend and fellow scholar, Matthew Bailie, had been the one to have notified me of the presence of supposedly long-lost scrolls in the local library. He had spent months translating these scrolls and we had exchanged numerous correspondence through letters and occasionally through telephones, debating the details. He was kind enough to impress upon one August Sullivan, the current head of Sullivan estates and library, to provide me unfettered access to these scrolls. Matthew was also the one to have leased this house before me. The house borrowed its name from the hill (which in turn bore the name of some explorer) and was locally called Cavendish House. Unfortunately, due to some unforeseen circumstances, Matthew had to rush back to his hometown to his family much before my arrival, and we hadn't corresponded since his last letter informing me of his decision.

On my first visit to the library, I was warmly received by Mr. Sullivan, who was anticipating my arrival. He spoke fondly of Matthew and narrated the story about their chance meeting at a convention that led to Mattew's invite to the secrets of his ancestral library. He then led me to a cordoned off section, kept behind thick doors and always under lock and key, with his wife Mrs. Sullivan, who was the head librarian, keeping a watchful eye from her desk. Before leaving, he too expressed concern about the well-being of our mutual friend and the loss of communication with him since his departure.

Once left alone, I browsed rows upon rows of ancient books and manuscripts, some foreign and untranslated, many tattered and moth eaten. Some had their covers torn off and some had burn marks, excessive creases or missing pages. Others, weathered so badly that it made their titles illegible. August, a product of modern times himself, had never bothered to read these and only kept these in the form of family heirlooms while maintaining the traditional secrecy and security of the books which was generationally inculcated among his family members.

I quickly breezed past all of them, as I had little interest in occult, mysticism or lore of witchcraft and dark magic. With a singular goal in mind, I made a beeline for the ancient scroll of Indic origin, looking for the unnamed scrolls pertaining to the "Dhaavak" or the runner. This was the only known original copy, the rest having been lost to time. Though 5 translated copies existed across the libraries of Europe, all of them were partial and most of them barred from public access.

Immediately, I started comparing the text with the information I had gathered so far through my correspondence with Matthew, making swift progress. It was remarkable how a 13th century handwritten Sanskrit manuscript from India had survived and arrived so far away to a distant land, the scroll itself being a copy of an even older series of texts. It was even more remarkable how it always led to persecution and was considered problematic enough for all later readers, translators and libraries to warrant hiding it or destroying it. Perhaps what was truly surprising was how frequently the runner was mentioned among much later religious texts from Tibet, Japan and also among some Slavic folktales. The later mentions were minor and fantastic enough to be ignored by any casual reader without making any cross-cultural connections.

I was buried in my work for an immense amount of time, until August walked in and broke my attention, impatiently pointing to the late hour of the day. While he had been generous so far to let me stay beyond closing hours, he did not budge on my repeated requests to carry the scrolls home. All my pleading was to no avail. I started walking out dejected, when a surprise greeted me. August handed me a thick diary that belonged to our friend. He told me it was left behind in the library after Matthew's departure and perhaps it may be useful to my research. With just one glance I saw it contained far more than where I had progressed so far, including information that was curiously, never shared with me. Elated, I took the diary and raced straight home to continue my research.

***

I dashed to my home and without any delay, started poring through the diary despite protestations from Francis, a caring old man I had hired to assist me with groceries and domestic help. I buried myself in the diary, ignoring most of the notes my friend had added, his progress and struggles in translating the scriptures. The need to validate my theory was the primary concern. A common history, a common myth, a shared fear held by many distant cultures across Asia and now I was going to be the first to establish its link to this continent. A vague cultural memory of a fear that came eons ago at a time mankind was perhaps unified and that it was all but forgotten today. Its remnants, now dispersed and divided globally, had turned into folktales and local legends fit only to grace children's bedtime stories.

Pages after pages of texts affirmed my long-held beliefs. The entity, mentioned carefully, with fear and reverence, had indeed been recorded in the Americas and at least two records existed of natives in Peru and Brazil dreading such a creature. But what was it? The only thing watered texts mentioned was that its domain lay among the stars. A cosmic sprinter of no shape or size. A void making its way through the vastness of space without any rhyme or reason. And lo- its last abode? It was right here, the woods around Helmsbury. This was where the latest entry was made. Where William Sullivan met the survivors of Henry Cavendish's ill-fated expedition. The accounts of natives who avoided this entire region were also recorded.

Added to the notes were newspaper cutouts about the big "event" of 1896 when one week, the town faced a sudden influx of certain peculiar individuals. Their arrival immediately sent alarm bells ringing among the hardworking and reputed townsfolk, when they started beelining into the depths of the forest. That night, the town filled with lightning strikes and fog while screams and chants emanated from the forest. A team of local law enforcement and villagers reluctantly entered the forest the next morning to investigate but found no signs of life in an area cleared of vegetation by artificial fires. Of what was found at the scene of the crime was never revealed, but un-named letters written to Matthew talked about dismembered bodies with some of the bodies displaying self-inflicted horrors too gruesome to write here.

The region which had already been shunned for ages even before its latest settlement, had now become a cursed and foul land to be avoided at all costs. Its groves, seen as a source of nightmares and terrifying tales, were now forbidden from even mentioning. No farmer, hunter or lumberer dared to enter, save for toiling near the shallow tree line. No farming or community events happened near the woods either. Lone carriages and motor vehicles passed swiftly and silently without halting and no one ever ventured for a late-night walk, especially outside town limits. The reservation of locals in talking to an outsider like me became clearer to me.

I was beyond excited at the effortless flow of information that was falling into my lap. So excited that I didn't notice the hours growing late. The runner, the dhaavak, the chaser among the stars, these were the only thoughts that filled my mind. The information about the entity was minimal, however consistent enough to link all various mythologies to one common ancestral source. As I skimmed through the pages, the notes ended abruptly, leaving a final bit of untranslated text and an ancient parchment pasted on to the page with just two lines, not written in any language I knew of.

I ran my finger on the rough surface of the paper. A sky filled with stars. A rock full of snow in darkness. *Dhaavak.* A forest in the dark. A hum in a cave. A large dark figure sang. *A runner in space.* I pictured vast desolate rocks on a distant world. A dark civilization of smoke and darkness. *Q'i'onel.* A bolt of

lightning tore through seas of magma. A million inhuman screams. A planet being ripped apart. *Dhaavak*. I felt my blood pressure rise. A sweat had formed on my brow. I felt feverish. I did not know what made me do it but I got up from my study desk, walked up to the window, as if in a trance and threw it open. I looked up at the sky and whispered softly,
"Dhaavak..."

****

Somewhere far away in a violent part of the galaxy, a swirling mass of dark cloud streaked across the emptiness of space, touching the surfaces of giant celestial bodies. It emitted a periodic pulsating blue glow while in flight and made its way across a hot gas giant. Crossing it, the mass coursed through a windy rocky world before entering immediately into the small moon that revolved around the green planet. The streak, unstoppable and leaving a long trail of black mass behind it as it raced across the moon, was about to jump into a floating galactic cloud of hot gasses when it started slowing down.

The mass swirled at the same spot in circles. Its journey was interrupted by a call, a pull. One cannot tell if the entity had any form of thoughts or feelings before it evolved into this cosmic form over eons, but it was very agitated at this gentle tug, an invitation. All it remembered was hunger. And hungry it had been, for decades. The call came from a familiar direction and this direction was associated with food.

The black mass turned and shot across the sky at impossible speeds. It streaked against a backdrop of a huge cluster of rocks lit by a distant foreign sun. Defying all laws of science, it raced hurriedly in one direction. Its destination – a pale blue dot of rock and water called Earth.

***

I was still standing at the study room's window, lost in the visions of the cosmic dance of destruction and creation when Francis walked in. "Master Matthew is at the door."

Surprised at the sudden turn of fate, I was about to respond when a sudden bolt of lightning tore through the sky and fell into the dark forest a few miles away.

The flash blinded us for a moment, turning the world silver and plastering our shadows onto the shining wall before they quickly dissolved back into the prevailing darkness in the room. A faint glow of yellow was visible before it extinguished and the forest returned to its eerie quietness. Our power instantly cut off; however, the town's sparse lights were still visible in the distance. We both looked at each other and shrugged curiously. I instructed Francis to light the lamps around the house.

Turning around, I left the room to find some candles and greet Matthew, leaving Francis to close the window. He was still peering through the glass, perhaps hoping to still spot any sign of a fire. Walking outside, I found Matthew with his back turned towards the house, looking into the forest. He seemed agitated, his gaze closely scanning the expanse of forest that lay in front of the house in the direction where the lightning had struck. A thick cover of fog was forming in the distance.

He turned to me and sternly asked, "Do you have my diary and my notes?"

"We thought you forgot it at the library so August allowed me to take it for safekeeping." I answered.

"You weren't supposed to read it. No one was. We cannot comprehend…"

"Comprehend what?" I asked impatiently.

"The terrors and the nightmares that have plagued me, the visions I have suffered from since I started reading these scrolls." Matthew answered. "If only I could describe my fevers, my ailments to anyone. The images that assail my dreams every time I try to sleep. The creatures, the deaths, the screams, the worlds so dreadful, so foreign." Matthew's lips quivered.

I tried to console my friend. He was very shaken and his eyes were red. He was dressed shabbily and a foul stench of alcohol assaulted my nostrils. His ramblings, while being utterly devoid of coherence, reminded me of the visions I just had before the lightning struck. I told him to leave his luggage in his car for Francis and come join me for dinner.

"We need to dispose of that diary first." Matthew said. "And fast, before your dreams are cursed like mine. Before something ungodly happens. We must-"

WHOOOOOSHH

A very sudden and strong gust of wind blew over our heads as we continued our conversation. It ruffled our hairs and made our collars flap in the wind. The candle in my hand immediately went out. We both looked up in surprise. The night air had returned to normal and the trees and grass stood still. There was no sign of a breeze, nothing swayed anywhere and nothing was picked up in the wind. The gust felt unnatural and out of place.

Eventually, without any explanation forthcoming, we

ignored it and entered the house. I called for Francis to come down and assist Matthew with his luggage but no response came. 'That old man. Lost in his thoughts again. Every damn time you need him.' I thought to myself, slightly irritated.

Leaving Matthew standing in the doorway again, I lit my candle once more and went upstairs looking for him. Ascending the stairs, I called out his name. No response. I made my way to the study and saw a lit lamp tipped over on the floor. *That was when my gaze fell on the body next to it.* And I let out a blood curdling scream.

On the cold floor Francis' body lay crumpled in a fetal position near the window. But that wasn't the inspiration of my scream. It was the state of his body. His body was completely shriveled, looking like life was sucked out of him forcibly, instead of leaving it on accounts of his advanced age. His lean body was now much leaner, stiff and unnatural. Veins burst out of the skin, his skin rubbery and his ribcage pressing out of his chest. Worst was his face. It was covered in a display of abject horror, bloodshot eyes bulging out and mouth gaped open. Even in a flimsy light, the end state of Francis was pretty conclusive. His life had gone, yet his body displayed no visible wounds.

I was still investigating the body when I had an uneasy feeling grow in my gut. Looking around in anticipation, I swept the room with my gaze. Empty. Then why this feeling? Finding nothing, I ran out of the room to go inform Matthew of what had transpired. The thoughts of getting the diary, let alone offering any hospitality, hadn't even crossed my mind in the face of this new development. Reaching the staircase, I halted after my very first step down. In my dash I happened to look back into the study. The now-erect lamp still illuminated the body, but something much more uncanny was happening that I had failed to notice earlier.

Outside the study room window near the body was absolute darkness, which by itself wouldn't be a curiosity, but here the darkness was subsiding. Slowly, this black mass, which was clearly distinguishable from the night's color, dissipated. Almost like a cover peeling off or a curtain being removed. Confused and clueless, I shrugged it as a trickery of shadows on my disturbed mind and continued going down the stairs to seek Matthew's assistance.

Downstairs, I found both my guest room and doorway to be empty. It wasn't too surprising; the door was wide open and I assumed my friend Matthew had gone back outside to carry his bags in. Cutting my way through the dark halls, I instinctively went outside looking for him.

Little did I know that a whole new world of celestial horrors awaited me outside.

Outside, I encountered my friend standing while facing away from me, looking into the forest. Still and soundless. I tried walking up to him cautiously. He started showing sudden signs of movement the moment I walked closer to him. His arms stretched out, almost inviting someone to embrace. He then let out a shrill scream, and laughed madly. Before I knew it, he started dashing madly towards the forest, arms flailing. His laugh echoed in the surroundings. I tried rushing after him but he had already gone inside the forest. My feet stopped at the sight of a menacing wall of trees in a curtain of blackness, opposing me. I could still hear Matthew's footsteps going further away from me.

That was when a wild cacophony filled the air with the most unearthly sounds that ever invaded my ears. Birds and animals screamed together. Adding to that was a scream. A human's scream. Matthew's scream. My concerns grew into shock when I caught that underneath this song of death and wailing lay a pulsating sound that rose and fell in repetition. The sounds reminded me of deep loud horns and elephant trumpets. Almost heralding the presence of something beyond my comprehension, something incorporeal that had aroused all the nightlife of the forest into a collective demonstration of terror. Something sinister. The noises set a great trepidation in my heart, making me fear for my safety, which was not entirely unwarranted. In the din and panic, I had already dropped the candle and was overrun with darkness.

The sounds slowly started retreating, letting silence encroach the ceded space. Then began the next wave of cosmic dance. A large black cloud rose up in the sky from the tree line, hiding the town's visible skyline and the last remaining artificial light source still available to me. The winds started blowing again, howling against the house. I watched, amazed and horrified as the clouds towering over me converged into a single mass.

I stood there in awe of this entity, watching it pulsate and emit glowing lights within it, unsure of my next action. The mass swirled in its position, forming a giant wall facing me. Its next move came soon, when it swooped down in my direction. My trance was finally broken and I turned and ran swiftly inside. A huge wave of black clouds swarmed towards the house, I slammed the front door and without catching my breath, dashed up the staircase. Finding refuge in my bedroom, I collapsed on the bed. I had no time so far to process my grief, my horror and my visions. My nerves soon calmed, and the realization hit me with full force. My friend was gone, Francis was gone, and now there was something here uninvited that had trapped me here, far away from civilization.

I was tired and afraid, my heart beating fast, my brain racing at an insane pace leaving no place for a coherent thought to form. A million thoughts formed and vanished, leaving me in a state of indecisive stupor. It didn't last too long however, for I heard a loud crash downstairs and I just knew my front door had given way to a supernatural force. I could hear the gushing of wind and clattering of objects below. A mad ruckus ensued in the house but it left everything on the upper floor un-touched. Once the winds and commotion died down, the house once more grew still, except now there were two occu-pants in it. The invader, which should have been a mere mass of weightless caliginous wind, made distinct noise grunts and footsteps as it searched for its prey.

****

I shut my eyes, focusing only on sounds. Soon enough, faint muffled sounds came from outside the door. There was a slight creak, as the locked door groaned from being gently pushed inwards. Then came another sound, the very gentle squeaking of the doorknob being turned. Af-ter two very gentle clicks and a tap, the knob returned into its place. Another soft thud echoed in the silence, indicat-ing a final forceful attempt was being made and then the sound of careful and muffled footsteps going down the

hallway; a sign of surrender.

"Damn right, not today." I smirked to myself as the attempts to open my door ceased. "You will not take me today."

I followed the sounds down the hallway, growing fainter and entering some room. This was my chance. Getting up, I got to my bedroom window and looked at the surroundings. Matthew's car was still there, as was a thick blanket of mist. The weather had suddenly changed, winds and lightning enveloped the forest and the town. My only hope to escape was to run out while my hunter was distracted, get to the car and pray it still functioned.

I opened my door slightly and looked around. The visibility was poor in the mist filled unilluminated house. Silence and gloom hung in the night. Stepping out, I stealthily made my way to the staircase landing. Time was of the essence and so was stealth. Unfortunately, my plan was foiled instantly. I turned around and witnessed an aggressive cloud come hurtling towards me. The sheer sight of a massive unnatural smoke covering an entire hallway filled me with dread. The pace at which it moved left me no time to get to the stairs. Without thinking, I dived into the study, the room closest to me.

The entity nearly scraped my fingers in the process as I tried shutting the door, recoiling as the door shook wildly. But in this one single contact, my brain was again filled with visions of a strange world in a very dark part of the galaxy devoid of stars. Dark desolate worlds full of lightning, fire and winds. Ancient sounds and civilizations one can only encounter in dreams. Strange swirling voids and blackholes, monstrous luminous plants and balls of smoke that defied gravity. Fast moving black clouds passed through skies emitting pulsating lights. Screams of humans filled my brain. But I felt something more. I felt what this invader, this ungodly creature felt. I felt his anger, his curiosity and his hunger. And I was his meal.

The violence had ended and everything was calm again. The creature had backed off and wandered off into some corner to ambush me again. I knew this thing was toying with me. For did it not effortlessly rip apart my front door? I reluctantly came to the same conclusion as this cosmic monstrosity already had – my escape was not possible. My demise was a matter of when not if.

If someone blames me for giving up too easily, so be it, they hadn't seen the horror, the visions, the deaths that I had.

I slumped on my chair in surrender. My gloominess had overtaken me. The bleak visions had made me feverish. I looked down. Francis… He was still here. Not a fate any man should meet. His silhouette was clearly visible on the floor from the tiny lamp I had left behind earlier. This room was my last refugee, the very room where I so foolishly invited this otherworldly horror into our domain. I sat at my writing desk and looked out the window. The town still slept peacefully, not knowing what horrors had transpired today. I knew what I had to do, perhaps the only thing I could. I positioned the lamp closer.

***

"In a world of dreams, conflicts, love and anger, the events of tonight will never leave a mark. But the world had changed, there was a guest among us. The woods around Helmsbury were once again the abode of something

sinister. It was banished once by methods and knowledge held by ancestors, now long lost to us in sands of times. But now it was back. It was comfortable and hungry; but the food was plenty. It will prowl this forest for food in perpetuity. Any victim unfortunate enough to come across it in the deep woods particularly in the night, for it prefers isolation and darkness, has my sympathies. But how long before it feels the hunger and sets out of his new domain to feed? I have set off the cat among the pigeons, and now I will pay for my sins. I can only hope one day someone gets to read this diary even though I have no clue how to get this diary out. Oh, the time has run out. It comes for me. The window… The windo…"

"I think we made a big mistake coming here." Tommy said, holding a diary.

"Dude, put that thing down and come check this out. What do you think this will go for?" Jack held up a vase.

"You don't understand, this diary… this is why they warned us from coming here." Tommy replied.

"Yeah, yeah, something happened, someone died 60 years ago. Big deal. Now put it down and find something valuable to take." Jack said as he shoved the vase in his backpack.

"But there has to be a reason why no one ever comes here. Why do they get angry at the mention of this place and the forest." Tommy protested.

"Are you going to keep talking or are you going to get something done? We are already here and it's getting dark. Let's grab something and get out before anyone notices. I am going back up there to look." Jack replied and then hurriedly rushed up the stairs back into the first room. The same room where Tommy had picked up the beautifully bound diary a few minutes ago.

Tommy looked around for a bit, gathering a few decorative plates from the display. The house was unassuming, mostly derelict, boards and panels littered the ground. Windows were broken, glass was everywhere. A thick layer of dust covered every inch of the house. The house had been empty ever since its previous occupant passed away, and no one in the town ever really talked about that night, save to give out vague warnings about the scenes they found.

"Hey come up here, look what I found. This pen looks expensive… What is tha…?" Jack yelled from upstairs.

"I am coming, Jack. Jack?" Tommy called out for him. Not getting a response, Tommy ran up the stairs and, in a few steps, reached the room. It was an old-fashioned study room, few shelves with books covered a wall. There was a cupboard full of stationary. A desk and chair were placed next to the window. It was the desk from where Tommy had casually picked up the diary on his previous round around the house. Standing on the window, looking outside was Jack.

"Jack?" Tommy called out as he walked cautiously to Jack. Jack didn't reply or acknowledge him.

"Jack?" Tommy called to him again, this time louder. Again, no response came.

Tommy got closer and gently placed his hand on Jack's shoulder. Instantly Jack's body collapsed lifelessly onto the floor as the legs buckled. Tommy panicked and turned the body around. Jack's face was dried and shriveled, with a grim expression of pain and fear etched onto his face. The eyes were bulging out and the tongue was swollen. The veins inside his pale thin neck were popping out. Only conclusion to his facial expressions was one of encountering extreme horror, which still didn't explain the mummified face. It was like someone had sucked out his life force. Even then, the window was shut tight.

Tommy looked outside the window. The sun had set already but the light remained. He noticed something unnatural happen. Thin strands of dark smoke gathered from every corner of the yard and forest, spinning and weaving into one mass. The mass grew larger and larger, swirling wildly. Winds gathered pace, making the trees sway. The large black void was now spinning wildly in front of the house. A veil of fog descended quickly over the area, covering it like spiderwebs. Tommy looked on, mesmerized, at this wild celestial dance. Lightning began striking in the forest, producing loud deafening noise. Yet, the void's spinning got faster and faster. With the increasing speed, the orb started pulsating with a warm blue glow.

Tommy was terrified, but he was being pulled, almost hypnotized. He could not avert his gaze. His brain started showing him visions. Visions of fires, of asteroids, of rives of acid and desolate planets entirely filled with water. Vivid images of humans being dismembered, being torn apart and their cries of anguish filled him. He felt their pain, and he felt the intent of this entity. Still, he couldn't move.

Tommy felt a tug from within. His skin started squeezing him. His eyes bulged out. Breathing became hard. He felt his life getting sucked out of him. The thing spun swifter, feeding on his prey from afar. Tommy let out a gut-wrenching scream, but no one was there to listen to his plight for miles. His scream echoed over the dense forest. Soon the screaming stopped, the winds stopped and everything fell silent. The crumbling house was left alone once more, standing as the sole witness of these dreadful events as the pigeons, mankind, carried on unawares.

The Prisoner Of Happiness

I sat calmly, dangling my legs off the cliffside, soaking in the warmth of the sun as the gentle breeze from the sea caressed my face. I took it all in, lazily enjoying the day. I listened to the gentle song of the waves and the chatter of nesting seagulls. The salty sea breeze saturated my lungs. My life couldn't get any better than this.

'I am happy! I hope I can stay this happy forever.' It was an unrealistic and childish dream perhaps, but no matter. Mr. Bradley had finally recognized my dedication at work and had handed me a major project. About time. I gave 12 years to this company. Oh, and we recently bought the house my wife always talked about! The house was close to the great white cliffs, looking majestically over the sea. This must be a dream. Has to be. Don't wake me up if it is. Everything that could, was going in the right direction.

Musing at the scenery, I unwittingly started walking towards the road. Not sure why, my legs took me there, I was too happy to be bothered and I had time to kill. Here, in the front of the house was a lawn marked by a huge oak tree at the edge of road, a hedge on the left covering driveway and on right was Catherine's dream - we had begun planting Dahlias, Tulips and

Berries. Rock Samphires and Galium plants graced the empty fields beyond the hedge, located wildly on cliff side and plateau. The area was devoid of houses save ours.

Beyond the lawn was a road that gently came down the hill, from the village tucked behind the low white hillocks, five miles away and dropped downhill out of sight after two hundred meters, going towards the town. I stood under the oak tree, shaded from sun and started to whistle. It is there I saw a curious sight that would change my fortunes forever and haunt me for the days to come.

There, under midday sun, with an unusual gust of wind, came flying a red cloth. A simple, ragged, dirty red cloth. Small, square, thin, no larger than a towel. Hovering swiftly over the road, coming from direction of the hills. Bewildered, I extended my arm as it came in my direction and effortlessly grabbed it.

I don't know why I even tried catching it, I guess it was my reflex action trying to take down a sudden flying threat that suddenly flew into my face unannounced. Then as swiftly as it came, I let it go and out it went fluttering away in all its glory. It quickly went out of sight behind the house and presumably off the cliff towards the vast sea.

I looked around for the source and sure enough, a very old black car passed me by swiftly. I couldn't see the driver, but in the back sat a very old lady, who was looking at me with a big smile as she trained her eyes at me. Next to her sat a young girl who seemed sad, almost on the verge of tears. The old woman kept looking at me, turning her head towards me as the car went further away, until her face was no longer visible. Eventually the silhouette of the car dipped out of sight on the sloped road to the town.

And that was it.

Dreams are not everlasting, are they?

Many days went past, and I didn't give it a second thought. Meanwhile I had struck off buying my dream car from my ever-diminishing list of life's goals. Too much good was happening too quickly and I was relishing every waking moment of it. Until one day…

I was tending to my garden, while Cathy had gone off to the town for work. It was a normal windy day with clouds turning the horizon light grey mid-morning. As I finished, wondering whether to answer my client's calls blaring inside the house just yet, someone's car came to a halt at the driveway. It was Steven, who owned the local grocery store. I had a good rapport with him. Awkwardly enough, the poor fellow walked solemnly and sadly, eyes red and face sullen.

"I have been trying to reach you."

"You alright, buddy?" I said, concerned now.

"Something has happened. There has been an accident… Cathy… She…"

***

The next few days were a blur, I have no recollection of anything since her funeral. I zoomed past my chores, avoided interactions and refused work. These walls are my cells now, they are slowly killing me. Darkness inside my heart and outside in home, and my light has left me. Why was my happiness interrupted so rudely by fate? I had it all, loved it all. Why me? I was grateful for all of it, wasn't I? I deserved that happiness.

It is etched in the cruel laws of universe for it to move ahead even if you don't. It is also a lesson in life for one to emulate and so with a great baggage I eventually started crawling again. With some difficulty and with a mind made up to honor her memories, I picked up the crumbs of life where they were left. I have to keep her memories alive, keep her garden alive, keep her house radiating with warmth. I have to be happy again... for her.

How was I to know my happiness had been cursed for perpetuity?

***

"Remember the old woody?" asked Harris, my longtime friend.

"Yeah, what about it? I asked.

"Okay so don't get too excited but I think I found a guy who could fix it with custom made parts."

"Do it!" I nearly yelled in excitement. "Whatever he charges. Get it done!"

Finally, a moment in what seemed like an eternity where I found some genuine happiness, something that overshadowed my pain for moment, relegating it into a very deep corner of my numb heart.

The good old woody was a family heirloom that I had nick-named as a child. It was a clock belonging to my great-great-grandfather, passed down through generations. Old woody had a sleek polished teak cover box, a silver pendulum and a black paint coat. It had intricate carvings and brass fitting on the edges in spirals. Unfortunately, it had lost some gears and had sat disused under my father's care. The thought of it breaking under his care had always pained my old man but now was the chance to fix it. In his memory.

The news had great effect on my health, and I excitedly counted down the days to its arrival. A childish innocence, and I daresay, a much-needed respite. Soon it arrived, delivered to me with extreme care by Harris, who knew of its importance to me.

The clock looked splendid, elegant, royal and old. The beauty, the history, the emotions it stored. We set about hanging it on the wall where it may be best displayed, especially to the guests. Tonight, I will sleep soundly...

A flutter

A sound of flapping cloth in the wind

A red cloth

whispers

'Not your fate'

'NO'...

CRASH

I woke up with a start. Out of breath. Sweating. Was I dreaming? What was it I was dreaming? I could not recall. Did I just hear a crashing noise?

I got up. I must check this late-night ruckus. Armed with a flashlight I walked out to find the source of noise, if I wasn't dreaming still, that is. What was I going to find? An intruder? Animal or man? A demon of my dreams? A scare out of my grandmother's tales?

Stealthily, I walked around the house, my eyes attentively scanning the darkness. Peering into nothingness for some motion. Everything was buried in darkness and silence. It was as if the whole house anticipated a commotion. Finally, I reached into the guest room. And an unpleasant sight greeted me.

On the wall, was a single screw, half outside the wall. Another empty screw hole next to it. On the floor was... the old woody... Dead. Gone. Done. A loose screw lay next to it. Must have come off. The clock was shattered into a thousand pieces. Unrecoverable. A hundred and fifty year of sentiments and history. Dust now.

I froze, paralysis set in. All that excitement. My happiness... I tried to wrap my head around it but to no avail. My thoughts exploded incoherently and then collectively fell silent.

As my numbness turned into tears, I felt something. A gaze. Something sinister. Terror started setting in as my heart started beating faster. I looked around but only emptiness and darkness greeted me. It was just a feeling but it was potent and solid.

Gathering courage and a kitchen knife, I searched entire house now, turning lights on. I double checked all the bolts and latches, only to find them all properly shut. Finding nothing, I left the mess as it was and retired to bed.

Once again, my happiness had been snatched from me.

***

A week later, much of which passed like a sand out of palm, I gathered the energy to go around the town for grocery again. Having faced multiple setbacks in a matter of days, I set out to find at least some semblance of normalcy in my life back.

The trip itself was rather uneventful, what really bothered me were the faces of my acquaintances. The same sullen look, silent treatment as if their tongues were too scared to say anything that may dig up fading memories from a box buried in the earth. The lip biting, a clear look of confusion as they scrambled to find words to greet me with. The eyes, loudly yelling of sympathy, none of which I had asked for.

As I was in loading up and smoking by the boot of car, I was approached by my car dealer, Brett.

"Hey, uhh..." he stuttered. "I heard what happened to Cathy and I..."

"Skip it." I said, not trying to sound polite.

Clearly flushed, and turning red he said, "I just wanted to let you know, remember the Swansons folks? They are doing some promotional stuff and offering new plans. I can try to pull some strings and get your car fully insured; dirt cheap with a better plan... You don't need to do anything but sign. It's the least..."

"Thanks." Feeling nearly guilty, I shook his hand and took his leave citing paucity of time. I actually needed that. Both the socializing and the insurance, having strained my finances by avoiding work due to the recent events.

I was glad to have wrapped up my trip quickly and pleased to have left behind those people, who in best of intentions were still unwittingly treating me like a creature from circus. I hurried back, trying to escape the forced socializing in 'a town the size of a mouth, where a tooth knew every other tooth' as my grandpa always said. (Yes, his ramblings never made sense even after I grew up).

Driving back, I was greeted by reminder of strong gale warning and an advisory to stay inside against the upcoming 100 kmph winds on radio. I thought 'Fine by me.' Curiously enough, as the horizon darkened in an as yet early evening, and my heart started getting heavier, I noticed something.

The roads were rightly empty and I was nearly at the end of town, moving towards the slope of hills behind which at a distance lay my destination, but here I saw some posters. Plain, artsy, colorful and upbeat. At every few streetlight posts, same posters: "Do you want to be Happy?" 'Yes, I do. For-ever.' I thought.

From what I could gather, intermittently looking and read-ing (while driving and squirming to read in a forever blackening evening), it was merely an advert for some job assistance cen-ter, not worthy of any further attention. I chuckled at the irony of it. 'How fitting. Just what I need, nature sending me signs.'

I could not contemplate the meaning of such an obsessive display, beyond grave financial want, that anyone would print so many posters and flood the empty, sparsely populated street go-ing till the edge of town.

I reached the house just as the winds were starting to pick up, rushing in against a barrage of chilly wind and cold drizzle that had just begun. The evening sky was getting darker than a winter night in the polar regions now.

I ran inside, removed my utterly damp clothes and had a hot bath. My meals were now just a duty I needed to do to survive, ever since Cathy... I no longer paid any attention to the timing, taste, quantity or regularity of my meals anymore. I settled into my bed, still hungry but cozy. Warmth soothing me under the protection of my covers. Power was gone by now and rain was dancing with thunders. But I could not sleep. I laid in bed, star-ing, listening intently to the songs of winds.

Howling, singing, wailing in tongues alien but tranquil none-theless. Every once in a while, the whistling of the winds would peak and my house would shudder, with a terrific intensity that would announce the arrival of doomsday and threatening to rip apart my house, timber and all, only to subside for next few moments as if to gather breath for next run at my house.

Then unexpectedly, came a loud noise, a creaking sound and a metallic thump. Like a hundred imps yelling together. I got up startled, and fiddled with the covers. The sound was somehow not so utterly outlandish and I had a hunch where the source was. Dashing through corridor, I arrived in the entryway, all dark and still, despite the nature's tantrum going all around me.

I peered through the window into the realm of darkness outside. Nothing was visible, no source of illumination either. What was left of this late evening was drowned in the ruckus of pitter patter of rain, a howling raging wind and deafening thunder.

All I could figure out was something loud was happening outside, in the cover of the dark environment. I had a sudden feeling of dread in my gut once again, a feeling of an unearthly presence. A feeling of being naked to an intense gaze. It wouldn't go.

Exactly at that moment, a sky shattering thunder raced by, quaking the house and rattling all the windows. The intensity lit the sky like bright daylight momentarily. That light was adequate to display the world, bathed in silver and black and what I saw was enough to send me in despair and shock.

I found out that the source of those noises was my car! I had forgotten to bring it inside the garage. And the oak tree, now uprooted by assault of nature, lay cleanly on my car, crushing it beyond the semblance of any shape or design that was once full of straight lines, fancy curves and sharp angles.

"Sorry, this is too soon. I just applied. Your insurance was supposed to come into effect from August. I..." uttered Brett.

"Thanks, it was a long shot anyway." I replied cutting him off and hung up.

A Late Night Fright

Do you even want to be happy?
'No.'

***

By now I had resigned myself to these barrages of unfortunate events. The world did not have happiness for me. Why should I be happy? What for? I do not deserve this wicked word. No affection, no hope, no goals. Just a dream of getting through to the next day without any disaster and cut my losses.

Maybe I am going mad. Maybe the world is. But wait, the world always was mad. The happiness is after me. It wants to take me back. To a world of gloom, where I belong. After regaining my senses from the shock of my loss, I treated myself with a self-imposed blockade, and successfully isolated myself from the common din of human activities.

I had fully committed myself to tending my wife's dream garden, both in an attempt to keep her in my mind and to keep my mind away from the horrifying acts of fate; but also to keep the weeds away from our precious plantations.

I was tending to our Dahlias and noted something peculiar. The flowers had developed brown spots and were rotting. I cut the affected branch and moved over to the berries. Brown. Freckled. Dirty soft patches. I checked a few more. Fungus. Mold. On all of them. It is then my head started feeling lighter, the implications of this, the consequence, I don't want to lose my Cathy's memories. I composed myself and rushed to the phone.

"Yeah brown, moldy and rotting. That's Botrytis Blight alright." answered Thomas, my plant nursery guy.

"What should I do?"

"Well, there is not much you can do, just cut out the infected branches and hope for a miracle. Come over and I'll give you a spray to kill the fungus, but most of it... It will be gone."

"Thanks."

That was the answer. I knew what needed to be done. It was simple. I can't have happiness; happiness won't have me. I got my shovels and the rake. It's time. Without any thought or remorse, I set out to work. The entire garden goes...

Later when I sat down for a brief rest, I once again felt the same dread, the same chill down my spine. The dread of being watched. I felt like someone ran their ice-cold fingers over my spine. I got up and looked around.

Nothing. Shrugging it off, I went to work again.

Hours later, I stood tired in the wet mud. Sweating. Itchy. Peering over the graveyard of multitudes of trees and plants. Those dahlias, Cathy got them herself. I didn't like them but she did. Those tulips were mine. Begonias, we planted those last March.

Our children... Now was the time to dispose these relics of my broken dreams. I carted the crushed vegetation and started dumping them off the cliff. One trip after another, until I saw *it*.

A visual too simplistic and too confounding to me. My eyes bulged out in sheer disbelief. Hanging from the cliff just below my house's ledge was a cloth. A simple red cloth.
The same old red cloth.

Somehow the cloth had been caught by the bush under the ledge and had survived the brute force of a storm. I leaned a little too out of comfort, tightly grabbing the railing with my life, pulled the cloth up and untangled it.

What is this and who are you?
Why did you choose me?
Are you the bane of my happiness?
An uninvited curse?
What is the meaning of this?
Who do you belong to?
Return my happiness to me!

***

I brought the cloth inside not knowing what to do with it. Maybe I intended to study it for ownership or history, I cannot recall. Putting it on my study desk, I intensely peered at it, turning it over and over, checking the corners and borders for any clue, label or embroidery. Red muslin. Light as a feather. Still as dirty and ragged as it was before. No markings of any kind which was disappointing. My concentration was soon broken by an unlikely sound.

A rattle. A very faint rattling noise. Like a glass or marble ball, perhaps a rolling glass bottle. Coming from either the corridor or the kitchen.

I was alert now, and quickly made my way from corridor to kitchen. There it was, a salt shaker, the offender, gently resting on the floor after rolling, I guess knocked down from edge of the counter by wind and gravity conspiring in unison.

I smiled. 'You are losing it.' But before I could leave, once more, the inexplicable dread assaulted me. The strong feeling of a presence, a watcher, a nefarious shadow somewhere behind me.

I decided to check my house for intrusion, in case someone

finds my money too appealing to possess by use of force. Maybe I wanted to know how the salt shaker ended up on the ground in the first place. Did it really fall by itself?

I started winding my way down the corridor, snaking through the rooms, taking care to check whether every single room's windows were bolted or not. Stepping into every brightly sunlit room, every shadowed and curtained room, peering under the beds and into closets, looking at window bolts, securing them and the door behind me after the 'all clear' sweep.

At all times did the feeling of dread clung to me viciously, draining my strength and filling me with most cruel self-doubts. Confused and demoralized now, I returned to my study room and looked at the cloth, before a thought struck me like a lightening.

My mind returned to the first day it all started. The day I first encountered this cloth. How it came flying to me. And worse. I remembered the car, it's occupants. Their faces. The crying woman and the old lady who grinned at me devilishly. Who were they? What was their purpose? Did they pass off a curse on me? Was I an intended victim? Were they themselves a victim of that curse? Something that was unwittingly passed onto them? But is the curse even real? Am I the subject of some wicked game?

I screamed in anger and frustration. No answers!!!

I have become a slave of my own life.

A victim of my fortunes.

A puppet of the fates.

I am... I am... *A prisoner of happiness.*

I was in the midst of my laments when an idea struck me, I didn't think it through, I did not consider any alternatives and

I did not wait to execute. A comic idea at best. I pulled out my lighter. Held the cloth higher. And set the cloth on fire...

I saw the flames climbing up, so I proceeded to dispose it somewhere. However, to my surprise, the flames quickly leapt up, readily consuming the cloth in hunger and wrath, swiftly devouring it.

Finding no time to react, my hands dropped it, reeling from the heat. I looked with horror and amazement at the swiftness with which flames spread, like a fiery flower, and covered my desk and chair.

As I watched the scene unfold, standing still, not registering the danger of the fire and clueless of the consequences, I felt goosebumps. The same old sense of dread. My heart started beating faster. I looked into the raging fire and finally saw the intruder, as clear as day.

In the burning room, standing behind the flames stood a figure in the far corner. I don't know where he appeared from. Unfortunately, it had no describable features save it was humanoid in shape and taller than me. It was just a faint transparent grey shadow that flames only gently licked. Evidently, the heat didn't bother it, as it never moved. I stood there watching for a few seconds until flames hid him momentarily and he was gone.

In my opinion, it was with my pure luck or bad luck, did I ever manage to spot the intruder, the stealer of my happiness. Presumably the being, a manifestation of my now cursed joyous existence, itself did not wish to get detected, until it had leeched off everything positive from my life. I now am inclined to think this is what the cloth brought and this is what the source for that young lady's tears and that old woman's smile was.

I found it prudent to run leaving everything behind. The house no longer mattered. There was no saving it now. The flames had already spread beyond the room. I got out and then locked the door, aiming to set alight the intruder if he could be burned at all.

"That's right, I got you. Burn."

I sat in the lawn, watching flames tower tens of feet towards heavens, black smoke bellowing through windows. I can't define my feelings of the moment, it was satisfaction, pain, anger jumbled into one.

I saw with bated breath as my memories, love, everything I held dear vaporized. I felt oddly content. My intruder, my happiness, the red cloth, gone. Burned. Ashes.

Whilst I sat there, watching the flames subside, firetrucks sounding their alarm at a distance, all thanks to the tower of smoke rising beyond the horizon. No one close enough to pay any attention to me yet. My happiness and my nightmares. Over.

I felt cheated by life and nature. But it all ends now. Suddenly, I felt a hand at my shoulders, and I was absolutely shocked to the point of jumping. I turned to face the visitor, angered by the distraction and flustered by my stupid reaction.

"Yes? Who died now?" I asked bitterly and in a sarcastic manner. It was a postman, horrified at the scene and taken aback by my response. He clearly meant to question my health and the situation but evidently decided against it.

"Well, I have a post for you." he replied, turning red.

I snatched the post and sent him on his way, tolerating no further distractions. It was a letter and a legal document. A will.

"Dear Mr..... to inform you that your uncle Oliver Haimes of Kent.... passed away last week.... On careful reading of his terms and a search for his immediate family members, we found you to be the nearest surviving next of kin. As such, do kindly meet up at the earliest possible date, with appropriate documents and identification so that we can initiate the proceedings for the transfer, as stated, among other possessions and savings, his mansion in Kent valued at EIGHT MILLION, SIX HUNDRED AND THIRTY THOUSAND POUNDS STIRLING at current market price..."

This timing of this letter, and the irony of my words spoken to the poor postman came rushing to my brain. I fell to the ground, bitterly weeping, tearing my hair.

In my sobs and wails, I noticed something out of the corner of my eye, a sight so cruel, I lost all the remaining vices of sanity. I saw, buried among the rubble, soot and golden hot timbers, a red cloth... Untouched by fire.

Did the happiness die?

I think not.

Happiness cannot be killed.

For, did the letter not prove it again?

My happiness lives, the joy stays, the delight flourishes.

My fortune thrives.

And if they do, I cannot.

Then what should I do?

There is no escaping happiness.

But if I can't escape it, what then?

Well, I will just kill myself then, I guess.

At The Count Of Twenty Three

"It's your turn!" Ryan protested. "I went last time."

"No, it's Shawn's turn." Noah pointed at Shawn.

"Fine." Shawn scowled at Noah and stormed off.

"And count slowly!" Alina chimed in.

Shawn glared at the group as he walked away to count till fifty. His destination was the boundary wall of an old abandoned warehouse right across the road.

"ONE" announced Shawn's voice.

Immediately the group off broke off and ran. Mike was first. He was also the fastest sprinter among them and by the count of four, he was already well hidden behind a dumpster.

"FIVE."

Alina ran and dived into the gap under the playground slide. She squeezed under the frame so well that she wasn't even visible from the sides.

"NINE."

Noah ran the farthest. Reaching the far end of the park, he jumped behind the bushes.

"FIFTEEN."

Ryan was left behind. He ran around looking for a spot. He tried crouching behind a bench but he was too exposed.

"TWENTY."

Frustrated, Ryan ran to the locked supply shed near the park gate and hid behind it.

"TWENTY-THREE."

Few minutes passed. Alina carefully scanned her surroundings. She could clearly see Ryan and Mike from where she was hiding but Shawn was nowhere to be seen. She giggled. Success! She slipped back into her hiding spot.

The early evening sun was getting low but it still gave warm radiance in the cool weather. The winds casually blew up leaves and deposited them elsewhere. In such an early evening like today's, the park and the streets were still empty, the parents were busy with their work. Entire neighborhood was silent and the only sign of life were these children playing hide and seek.

Few more minutes had passed when Ryan appeared, scratching his head. "Guys, where did Shawn, go?"

At first, no one answered, but seconds later Alina popped her head out. "Shhhhh. Are you crazy? He is trying to get us to come out!"

"But I don't see him anywhere!" Ryan replied.

"What's going on? Why aren't we playing?" Noah came out of hiding to check out the gathering.

"Shawn is being a goofball. He hid from us." Alina answered.

"But it's his turn! Let's go find him." Noah said.

Everyone nodded in agreement and the group started marching from the park to across the street, where Shawn was supposed to be counting against the wall. Mike saw the group pass by him and came out of his spot to join them.

"I could see you! Stupid place to hide." Alina laughed again.

"I was the last one so I win." Mike responded, making a face at her.

"Well actually, Shawn isn't here. So, you didn't." Ryan said.

"Where is Shawn? He was supposed to look for us." Mike asked curiously.

"He is hiding from us." Noah replied, making a bitter face.

"When we find him, we are telling him he can never play with us again." Ryan added and called out his name. "Shawn!"

Shawn didn't respond to them. The group followed the boundary wall of the abandoned warehouse across the street, looked around the corners and at one point they even tried peeking inside through the gates. They called out his name many times. But still no sign of Shawn.

"Maybe he went home?" Mike asked.

"Without telling us?" Noah responded.

"Maybe his mom called him?" Alina also added.

"He should have told us before going home." Noah complained again.

"Guys, forget about him. Whose turn is next?" Ryan asked impatiently.

Thus, the consensus was reached quickly. The game will continue without Shawn.

"Who goes next?" Ryan asked again. "Because I did before Shawn."

"Mike!" Alina interjected and grinned.

Before Mike could protest, everyone nodded. Mike stormed off to count, fuming and mumbling.

The kids split up again to hide.

None of them noticed the strange figure that now occupied one of the benches

in a far corner of the park.

***

"Alright. I am counting now. ONE." Mike declared.

The group was ready this time. They had already started running to their preferred spots.

"FOUR."

No one had seen Noah's hiding spot. He ran fast and back into the bushes he went.

"SEVEN."

Alina panicked momentarily. Everyone knew about the slide now. She turned and ran straight to the third bench in the park. She figured, the tree next to it would hide her from the side and out of Mike's sight. She also noticed that a weird stranger now occupied a bench far away in the park.

"TWELVE."

Ryan decided to go back to the supply shed. He will have to improvise now. He stood into a plant bed and pressed against the wall of the shed. His legs were covered by plants and his top half was masked by wooden frame of the shed jutting outwards.

"SIXTEEN."

Ryan took a deep breath. His location wasn't the best but he might not be the first to be detected.

"TWENTY."

Noah was ready to win this. But he will need a new location after this round. He was thinking about that.

"TWENTY-THREE."

Silence dawned in the park. Minutes passed. First one. Then five.

Frustrated now, Alina stood up and looked around. No Mike. Just a stranger on bench, still there minding his business. She brushed her knees and stepped into the open.

"Guys?" She yelled. "Guys come out. I think Mike ran away."

"No, he must be here!" Ryan walked out, trying to scrape the mud off the bottom of his shoes.

Noah poked his head out to fully gauge the scene. At first, he only saw a guy sitting quietly on a bench. But that was normal. Many people came to sit in that park daily, except today. Then he looked at his friends talking to each other in the open. 'Not again.' he thought, rolling his eyes. Noah stepped out of the bushes to join them and ask what had happened.

"Maybe he went home?" Alina asked.

"No way!!! His parents aren't home yet. He is staying with us till 8 P.M." Noah replied.

"Then, he must be hiding. He is teasing us." Ryan replied. He looked at the potential hiding spots in the park. He would have seen Mike come back into the park to hide. However, he did spot a lone guy sitting alone in the park. Ryan too, ignored that.

The trio gathered near the park entrance, looking across the road and scanning the deserted sidewalk. Not a single soul anywhere, Mike had vanished into thin air. They crossed the road once more, and followed the brick wall all the way to the corner. They peeked around the corner but all they saw was a desolate road going out towards the city. No one was visible for miles. The group turned back to where they came from, Noah in the lead.

"Where is he hiding?" Ryan asked.

"What exactly are we going to do now?" Alina was getting

slightly scared. Mike missing meant the parents would be mad.

"We tell my mom. She would know what to do." Noah tried his best to reassure them.

"Do we know what Mike was doing?" Ryan asked, getting agitated. He was following Noah closely.

By now Noah and Ryan had gone back around the corner, momentarily losing the sight of Alina.

"He was counting till Fifty, wasn't he? I think he was at Twenty-one. No! Twenty-Three!" Alina squeaked from the behind the corner, while she was still out of their sight.

"I know. But then he stopped counting." Noah reminded her.

"That's what I remember too." Ryan tried hard to recall any additional details.

The duo took few more paces before anyone noticed Alina hadn't appeared from the corner.

"Wait!" Ryan turned around and paused.

"What?" Noah turned his head while continuing to walk.

"Where's Alina?" Ryan asked in disbelief.

Noah immediately ran all the way back and looked around the corner. Sweat appeared on his brows immediately.

"She…She was right behind us." Noah's voice filled with fright.

"We were just two steps ahead of her!" Ryan was slowly feeling fear take over.

"I don't feel good about this, let's go tell my mom," Noah replied, visibly shaken. "I want to go home."

Without arguing, Ryan started quickly walking with Noah towards his house. He casually glanced at the park. It was empty. The benches were all unoccupied. Ryan was genuinely terrified now. His parents had taught him about talking to strangers and what they could do. Even though his parents rarely ever found time to play with him, they would be mad and never let him play outside in the park by himself again, if they found out what had happened.

Lost in thoughts, Ryan's pace quickened. Without realizing, he almost broke into a jog. He wanted to reach to safety as soon as possible. Noah followed his lead and tried catching up to him. By now, both were running full speed on the pavement along the wall. Ryan had the head start and was ahead. But Noah saw something Ryan didn't.

"Ryan, wait!" Noah yelled.

Ryan had no time to listen or react. All he saw was an imposing figure in front of him. The stranger from the park!!! He had crossed the road and now stood on their side of the road, blocking his path. His eyes bulged. The man's figure grew closer and larger. Before Ryan could stop himself or change his direction, he crashed into the stranger at full speed.

"Nooooooo." Ryan screamed at the top of his lungs.

***

Jeremy was impatient. He sat on the bench, tapping his feet involuntarily due to worrying. He looked at his phone again. The cab was still twenty minutes away. Disappointed at the information, Jeremy put the phone on his lap. This was not how he pictured his day was going to go. There was an important interview and a mix up with directions made him take the wrong bus.

Luckily, he realized early and after getting off in a quiet neighborhood, booked a cab from his phone. It would be costlier but

at least he would get to his destination. Hopefully, just in time. He then walked to a secluded and empty park, he had spotted earlier, to wait.

He clasped his hands and looked at the surroundings. The park was empty, except for a few children engaged in a highly competitive game of hide and seek. None of them looked older than eleven. Jeremy watched them run around like rabbits and reminisced of his own childhood. He mentally graded their hiding locations, remarking to himself at how he would have hidden better or found them quicker. Another thing that made him nostalgic was how parents had let these kids run around the neighborhood unsupervised, something that was commonplace in his era but it was very rare to see it in today's time.

Sixteen minutes passed by and Jeremy spent those alternating between his mobile apps, songs and watching the children play. He checked the arrival time of cab once more and heaved a sigh of relief when he saw it was just four minutes away. Turning his attention to the game, he noticed a few kids had gone home. The rest were walking on the other side of the road, talking. The game seemed over, as did his wait.

He stood up and stretched, grabbed his bag and after double checking his app, marched straight to the pick-up spot. He crossed the road to wait for the arriving cab. He had seen the children going around the corner and out of sight.

'Perfect. Will get there in time.' Jeremy thought, checking the time on the phone. He was still buried in his phone, when he stopped at the spot to wait for the cab. Suddenly, he heard a scream and before he could react, a kid sprinting fast ran into him, knocking his bag and the phone down.

Jeremy steadied himself and picked the kid up, before

bending down to scoop up his belongings. "I better not be late kid." He muttered under his breath as he checked his phone. It was scratched slightly but working. The cab was nearly there.

"Whoa slow down. What is going on here?" Jeremy enquired, as he now turned his attention to the kid that had ran into him.

"No…nothing, mister." The kid replied with a slight hint of panic in his voice.

The kid behind him had stopped screaming and had gone silent.

"Is that kid bullying you?" Jeremy asked, pointing to the now silent kid behind.

"No, he isn't! We were just playing." The first kid answered, still out of breath.

"Well, where are your parents?" Jeremy demanded.

"Please mister, we are just trying to get home!" The second kid responded.

During this entire conversation, Jeremy couldn't shake the feeling of certain familiarity. Something he knew he had seen before. He thought about it, trying to remember. Soon, an old memory tucked somewhere in a deep corner of his mind unlocked. He opened his phone's web browser mid-conversation and quickly searched something on internet. He looked at the kid near him. Then at his phone screen. Then back at the kid again. His eyes widened.

"My god. You… You are Ryan Davis. Do your parents know you are here? You were all over the news two years ago. The whole town looked for you." Jeremy stammered due to shock and disbelief.

"See? I knew it wouldn't work!" Ryan started giggling.

"But it did! We got him here, didn't we?" Noah answered,

laughing loudly.

Jeremy's face went blank with utter confusion.

"Let me call the police, they will take you to your parents!" said Jeremy, as he started typing the emergency number.

"No need, mister. Ryan loves it here." Noah replied in a serious tone. "Don't you, Ryan?"

"Ummmm… I do." Ryan thought about it and answered reluctantly. His face displayed a brief moment of panic and recognition. Like he was fighting to remember something.

"He gets to play with me all day, every day!" Noah added.

He looked at Noah to answer and his face went from showing confusion to one of abject horror. His heart almost skipped a beat. The kid he was talking to was no longer looking like a regular kid. Noah's skin had turned into a deathly shade of pale.

He looked skinnier and his skin looked moist. Worse, his eyes were entirely pitch black and Jeremy felt like he was looking into a bottomless well. Jeremy's sixth sense was blaring loudly. Noah's new posture exuded pure malice and sheer hatred. Yet Noah just stood still and peered intensely at him.

Self-preservation made Jeremy take a few steps back. That was when Ryan came into picture again. Ryan too, had turned into a black eyed, pale skinned ghoulish entity, now silently looking at him. He also made Jeremy fear for his safety. He kept retreating on the pavement, until he ran into an obstacle. Jeremy turned around swiftly and there was the girl he had seen before, playing hide and seek at the park. Her look was menacing. She looked just like the others, yet more dreadful. More vicious. Curiously, her dressing style resembled that of a late seventies kid.

He realized was surrounded, like a prey among a circling pack of wolves. He prayed for his cab to arrive soon. Instinctively he tried crossing the road to safety but to no avail. His feet stopped as he saw two more children smiling at him from the other side of the road. Their black eyes looked like shiny black beads from that distance. Their pale skin glowing in the setting sun's light. Jeremy was speechless now. His fight or flight response giving its verdict.

"I am very disappointed today, mister." Noah approached him, walking erect and sternly. His face displayed no emotion and his absolutely black eyes gazed into his soul.

"I get just one day every year to make new friends and this year was also wasted," Noah stepped closer to him. "I am sorry mister but you can't play with us. You are too old."

Jeremy was completely encircled in the middle of the road. He tried running through them but with a single push, Mike effortlessly threw him back into the circle, knocking the wind out of him. His phone went flying out of his hands and hit the pavement with force. The drooling children stepped closer and closer, taking their time. Their beady dark eyes grew closer as they pushed their snarling mouths closer to feed on him. Jeremy screamed until he could not anymore. His vision blurred. All he saw was eyes, those tiny little voids next to his face and fangs digging into him.

Moments later a cab arrived. The road was empty and the sun had already gone down below the horizon. The cab driver looked around and found nobody. He tried calling back his potential customer. After waiting for two minutes, he cursed and drove away. His car narrowly avoided crushing an abandoned phone on the road. The shattered screen on the phone was still lit, displaying a partial date... 23rd Augu...

A Nightmare In The Day

Sharon stepped onto a dusty street. It was a particularly hot day. She started walking with the deepest sigh a teenager could produce. Sharon was not too fond of the summer sun, she wouldn't be out, if she didn't have to.

"As if I am ever allowed a little time to myself." she whined. She continued dragging her feet, trying to find solace in shades of anything, even electric poles and street lamps.

Sharon was lost deep in music from her earphones and her thoughts. Thoughts mostly about hating everything. Her eyes a brilliant shade of blue, hair darker than the darkest nights.

It was all going fine. As fine as it could be. Sure, it was hot and sunny, but at least the Earth rotated just fine. And Sharon didn't like that.

That was until her mind wandered away from her complaining about the universe towards the nature of her surroundings. She noticed an emptiness around her. A sense of loneliness and alarm. There was no one to be seen, even on a busy afternoon.

She wiped a glistening bead of sweat off her forehead and clutched on her backpack tightly as she looked around, her shiny plastic wristbands reflecting a blinding flash in sunlight.
She was all alone in a market in daytime.

How is that even possible? Usually, this place is always bustling with hordes of office goers, school children, shopkeepers, taxi drivers. She noticed that because she hated it passionately, she hated the commotion and now there was nothing to hate!

Sharon pulled out her earphones. Music was replaced by eerie silence. She could hear the whistling of the wind, rustling of the leaves, scraping of the plastic bags on the pavement somewhere as wind blew them away, rushing water from a leaking pipe. Yet no one was there to engage, to tend to any of it.

What is it? What is going on?

The shadows!

Yes, the shadows looked weird.

She couldn't explain how, they were normal sized, faced the right directions yet much darker than usual. Almost like a badly added filter in a photo app.

Sharon may have not focused on the world so far after leaving her house, but now she was attentive. Her alarm bells were winding up to ring anytime. Something was definitely odd.

She looked around. The world was at a standstill. The stores and the cafes were open, with food and cups laid out. Cars were in line and ordered on the road. The only thing missing? No human soul. Not one body in the entire block was out visible. Yet, there was no sign of a chaos or hurry.

She stepped into middle of the road, not feeling comfortable with the shadows. "Really?" she told herself, feeling stupid. Yet her heart beat faster. The shadow of grass blades, the cars, bins, the emptiness, all looked darker and menacing.

Something was not natural. She couldn't pinpoint what was wrong. But something was triggering her sense of safety. The more her brain registered, the more scared she got.

She turned back, to go where she came from, making sure to stay in the 'burning' sunlight as the day grew slowly warmer. The shadows didn't feel comfortable to her even though she was still unable to convince herself about the reasons.

As she turned around, her attention was caught immediately by a movement out of the corner of her eye. Something moving underneath a car. She bent down and looked with caution. It was a cat. A scared kitty cat, hiding in the shadow accorded by the car.

Sharon tried to coax her to come out, she herself wouldn't go into the shadow now, would she? But the cat wouldn't listen. After some time and repeated attempts, she gave up. HOME was all what she could think of now.

She had taken barely one step further when she heard other sounds behind her. Something slithering and some low guttural sounds. A thick wad of slime splattered right behind her.

Sharon turned around, hastily.

The sounds weren't from the shadows, but a little higher, from the sky. Of course, the lights also cause the obstacles to birth shadows, don't they? The day was abnormally bright today. Abnormally hot too. The sun…

She looked up. Shadows contracted beneath her feet as sunrays changed their direction.

An exposure to blinding flash temporarily made her shield her eyes, so she was unable to see the golden and lava red tentacles emerge from the shapeless, formless source of bright sunlight hovering right above her, a few hundred feet up in the sky, covering the real sun behind it.

But her eyes adjusted quickly… ***AND HER FACE CONTORTED IN TERROR.***

The Lurker In Sight

The whole world seemed to swirl around in a frenzy. I looked at the scenery surrounding me. The silvery rays of moonlight, filtering between slumbering trees painted some of the most fantastic art in black and silvery white I had ever seen, an art that would make even the greatest of modern-day painters blush.

It must be my mind, playing its old games again, I thought. Any rational explanation of the unnumbered terrors I had witnessed over the past year, was desperately clung to by my mind.

The forest at night was so calm, peaceful, dark and haunting. The aroma of freshly dug earth, saturated by a downpour, stifled my nostrils. There were no sounds to keep me company tonight, no crickets, wind, creatures of the night or the vegetation. None. As if everything was on a standstill. It was too silent. Much too quiet for a deep dark forest full of life and it was unnerving. Yes, unnerving!

That means *she* is here. She is near! Where exactly? Doesn't matter. She is present everywhere! She is watching you, following you. Closely. In these thickets, the old ones say, in the dead of the night if you walk alone, she creeps up to you. The elders in town trembled in fear at the mere mention of her existence.

Don't go looking for her, they had warned me. And don't

surprise her. Should you be so unlucky to encounter her, you will get marked forever. She creeps up to you, slowly and steadily. With the feet of wind and patience of a slow river that cuts the rocks over millennia, she follows you. There is no escape. No there is not - just a long excruciating wait. The lurker will catch you eventually. She always does.

Tonight, I find myself here again. A year since *that* night. There has to be a way out of this nightmare. How did it ever come to this? That fateful night I was here - I regret ever doing that. Curses to that infernal night and to that accursed curious nature of mankind, my bane, my scourge - Alas! I was naïve.

Why did I willingly condemn myself so? The youthful curiosity had overwhelmed me. I went there against my better judgement. But local legends are beautiful, aren't they? And what do they say about legends? Aren't those just stories forgotten by vestiges of long-lost time where they once might have been true?

So, I in my folly, set out to discover the local legend, the LURKER, the lady in the woods, the timeless, ageless, unrelenting stalker, restless horror and an undefined terror, on a moonlit night. And that one decision cursed my existence forever.

I decided to spend that night at the same wretched place I find myself standing at tonight. I found it with slight difficulty, by walking on an abandoned, forgotten path that had been nearly reclaimed by nature. The path led to a ramshackle mansion abandoned eons ago, but that was not my destination. My goal was the graveyard next to it, and in it, a very particular spot hidden by greenery. I now understand why it was shunned by the locals.

Here, among the coppice, lay a very special tomb. Inside it, was an unmarked grave, the conclusion of my quest. A grave that was nameless, unloved, uncared, moss ridden, weathered and ravaged by vagaries of nature. The occupant was a woman, as betrayed by elaborate carvings on the stone and the mural. Is she her? My nightmare, my lurker, my follower?

I found myself mesmerized by scenic but tragic beauty and the irony of life. The grave spell bounded me. I sat there watching, utterly hypnotized, for what was an eternity. Then, I saw her....

Her. The woman. She was outside the tomb, behind a lone tree, looking at me, unemotional and with unbroken expressions, like she was a bust carved by Greeks of bygone era. A relic of some temple of Hera or a stolen treasure out of Delphi itself. But she was not. She seemed to be of flesh and blood. Yet, her face was reflecting the moonlight gently and her expressions frozen, like a porcelain mask.

Under the canopy filtered moonlight, I saw her pearly eyes, I swear by her dark red lips, her flushed blue cheeks, a beauty beyond compare. I sighed, and let a cold breath of longing, enamored by the seraphic beauty I had just witnessed. Finally, without a word she went behind the tree and then she vanished.

My life was not the same again after that night. I longed for her. And I dreamt of her. Little did I know that this was just beginning of my nightmares.

She follows me.

She follows me everywhere. You can never see her. But you can always feel her presence. Her watchful gaze. The blue pearly eyes of my lurker, the destroyer of my peace. When I retreat to my room, she is there at the end of the corridor, waiting. Looking at me from behind. You cannot see her if you turn around, for the corridor always turns up empty. But she is there. Looking

at me, expressionless, motionless. I am sure of it.
She stalks me.

I can sense her presence every time I leave my house. On the sides of this lonely country road where greenery is much thicker. She is watching me from the dense woods. Of that, I am convinced. Oh, her eyes, I could feel them burn me. These familiar woods no longer feel welcoming or friendly.

I remember the very first time I sensed her, which was on my first morning walk since that night. I paused, standing there filled with dread, unable to coax my fast-beating heart and my numb feet to go any further and deny the unseen. All my attempts were to no avail. I returned home swiftly, lest a passerby saw me terrified and frozen in middle of the road and subjected me to mockery for relenting to childish fears and fantasies.
She follows me everywhere.

In the market, behind that distant parked car, she has to be. I would know, for I swear I caught of glimpse of her gown, just a corner of it, appear from behind the cover provided by the car as if she hurriedly had stepped back to hide. She is never seen by anyone else; she makes sure that her paths are devoid of human eyes. She is shy and any unwelcome arrival makes her presence fainter until I can feel her essence fade away.
She is here.

I can feel her looking at me when I read my evening newspaper, peering intensely at me from a window behind me. I have tried many times to turn around faster or to catch a reflection of her in my silverware, but to no avail.
She loves mocking me.

Whenever I am engaged in any task, she walks by the door. Making sure she is "seen" in the swift passing moment out of the corner of my eye, greeting me with her faint perfume, a gust of wind and sudden inexplicable dread. I just know any of my attempts to look at her will be fruitless. Trying to catch a glimpse of her is a futile exercise.

She watches me.

When I retire to my bed, she watches me. I can sense her looking from dark corners. Every time I step out my door for a breath of fresh air, I am sure she watches me. There! I can feel her presence again. My spine tingles and sudden chills overtake my body. Beyond the garden, someone is behind those dancing branches among the trees, looking at me with a keen gaze, ruining my life.

The cause of all my sorrows. This is too much to bear for my weakened mind. For a full year have I watched and prayed for this hateful creature of pure evil to be gone from my life. But she never does. She loves tormenting me. But no more! Something tells me my time is at an end. My lurker will soon come and collect me. Come fulfill your curse, you wretched abomination. You cruel travesty of nature. Here I am, back to where it all started, one year ago.

Tonight, as I stood under the canopy of rain drenched tress, squishing on the fallen leaves and soil with my shoes, all I could hear was monotonous buzz of insects. She will be here soon, I reminded myself. It's inevitable. I lingered at that spot anxiously, with my heart pumping furiously unlike it ever did before.

Waited.

Listened.

Sighed.

And Lo- suddenly there was a blinding flash behind me. Finally! My end is here. My lurker, my unnamed bane, the stalking dread that escapes all explanations, is here. Take me and finish this harassment. I beg of you. As a mercy, end this game of hide and seek.

I turned to face it, ready to surrender. But all I saw was a lone policeman with a flashlight. My car parked at the start of the trail must have given my whereabouts away. The same trail which started at the borders from where this reign of madness began. He must have been patrolling the highway and probably witnessed my mad dash toward the old graveyard – the lurker's domain, and thought I was up to some folly or some foul play, and hence, followed me deep into the unknown parts of the woods.

As I attempted to explain to him my predicament - for I can only dream about how outlandish my story must have sounded to an unbeliever of supernatural forces that exist beyond the realm of our meager minds - I saw her.

She had arrived, half floating, her feet too gentle to adorn foliage or make a sound. She silently approached us, appearing behind the policeman. Ready for me. Ready to claim her prize.

My face must have shown vivid details of fright, as the policeman followed my horrified gaze, and turned around to face the source. Everything was so sudden.

There are some questions unanswered,

Some mysteries that remain,

Why did he have to follow?

Why did he interfere with my fate?

That night, he fell in my stead.

A young man who stood in her way.

And now,

HE CREEPS ME NIGHT AND DAY!!!

Kaleidoscope

"Mom, can I have a Kaleidoscope?" Glenn asked.

"What do you need a Kaleidoscope for?" Rachel asked in return, looking at Glenn with suspicion.

"I need it for my school project!" Glenn pleaded.

"You needed binoculars for your school project."

"But I did!"

"Yeah? Where are they now?" Rachel asked sternly.

"ummmmmmmmmmm…"

"Right."

"But mooooom!!"

"No Glenn, no. You know we cannot afford stuff. You don't even use them."

"But I will use it this time."

"Sigh. We can't, honey. Not until I get paid. And no more of this."

"Ha, Glenn gets no toys! nuh uh!!!" said his little brother Tim, sticking his tongue out.

"MOOOOOOOOOM Look at him!!!"

"Stop it Glenn, he's five. I am getting tired of you fighting him all the time." Rachel replied, trying to hide her frustration.

***

"Thank you, but… uhm… is there a cheaper alternative?" enquired Rachel, looking around and lowering her voice, as if the world was suddenly conscious of her financial woes. She never had to buy anything used before but now there is a house that needed to be filled and on a tight budget too.

"That brown sofa? How about that? Cheapest one I got. A bit torn on the left side cushion, chipped but nothing that can't be polished or sewn." Mr. Wilkins replied, trying his best to be genuinely sympathetic to her plight. He hoarded everything that the town discarded, in his shop.

"Uh no thank you! I'll take it as it is and get it polished, maybe next month?" Rachel replied, mortified at the thought of having extra expenses. "Also, could you please get it deliver… Glenn? Glenn, get back here and don't touch anything!"

Glenn, by now had wandered off far into the depths of that warehouse. Stacks on left and stacks on right in aisles, towering over him. Years of junk gathering dust, decades of town's collective history unattended, forgotten, neglected and forsaken, lay there. Toasters, tools, toys, kitchen and gardening equipment, rusty buckets and cracked photo frames but variety going all the way to royal lamps and shades, king size beds and wardrobes that probably escaped from museums.

Something pulled Glenn today, he kept walking on deeper and deeper into the building. He was scared of dimly lit rooms but today his legs didn't give up. He walked, exploring or rather being drawn in by the destiny, until he reached the end of the warehouse, till the last aisle, where lay a small box, and on top of that box lay an object, glistening under dim yellow bulb.

"Glenn, where did you run off to? I told you… What's that? No! I am not buying it."

"But mom, look! A Kaleidoscope!"

Mr. Wilkins squinted hard, looking curiously at it. Golden colored wrap over a brass cylinder, 10 inches in length, a glass eyepiece and a tinted glass cover on larger end. Heavy for a toy.

Curious. Very curious indeed. He racked his brain hard but he still couldn't recall where he got such an object from. His brain was running at full speed, sifting through his memories. Where? When? Was it antique? Valuable? He remembered his every purchase. Every, but surprisingly not this one.

"No, put it back where you found it, you know we can't afford it." Rachel whispered.

Never the one to miss a chance at making extra money, Mr. Wilkins decided rather quickly about it. Brass, heavy, thoroughly ruined paint scheme. Yeah, that will be sitting for long. Plus, he had a sudden feeling of pity ever since the family had arrived at his store. He felt sorry for what had happened to Rachel. She deserved a break.

"$5 for that, make the kid happy." 'That better not be a valuable piece, kid.' He thought.

Rachel looked at Glenn's twinkling eyes. He was just 12 but it reminded her of the first time she held him in her arms, a little bundle with big bulging blue eyes.

"Okay, but promise you won't lose it this time. Mr. Wilkins please write this up and oh, about the sofa, yes-"

Moments later a smiling and happy family walked out. As Mr. Wilkins watched them leave, his mind was still slightly questioning his snap decision. *What if that toy was actually valuable?*

Oddly enough, he suddenly felt lighter and cooler, as if a

huge weight had been lifted off him.

***

It was a cold and moonless night; the wind swayed the tree branches as they danced noiselessly to midnight's humming. A cool draft from window hit Rachel's feet. Windows open and every single light out. That's how she liked sleeping.

The creatures of shadows retreated to safety as Rachel suddenly woke up, nudged by a pang of thirst. She got up and reached dreamily towards the bottle at the bed side table. As she took her first gulp, her eyes were attracted by a sudden flash.

Was that a faint beam of light somewhere that appeared and went out quickly?

She waited for it to appear again.

A few seconds went by. Each as long as eternity.

Still, she waited.

Looking around. Her brain was no longer dreamy and her eyes were hypervigilant.

And she waited.

It's been a full 10 seconds now.

There!

It was unmistakable. A sudden bright flash of light rushed in from the slit under her door. It went out as quickly.

She carefully tiptoed all the way to the door and listened for any unfamiliar sound. At night any sound, save the ticking of the clock was unwelcome and hostile. More so now, that she and the kids lived alone. She opened the door and peeked out, first at the landing and then down the stairs.

Darkness. Pure darkness. Unadulterated darkness answered

her curiosity. Not betraying any source of light. What if some hostile force was looking back at her, using the same darkness as its refuge, biding its time patiently to reach out and lunge at her face?

Rachel stepped out warily and scanned her surroundings. She paused for a minute but no light returned. However, there was a noise now. Faint. Child-like. Down the corridor, from the direction of kids' bedrooms.

She tiptoed again as she went for the source. The murmuring continued. Her short quest ended at Glenn's bedroom. The light was much dimmer now, but still clearly visible from under the door. It kept disappearing every few seconds.

Whisperings too, were quite fainter now. But it was indeed Glenn's voice.

"Yes... But mom won't... No, I love these colors... Haha... What else... Symmetry... How did you..."

She walked in without a warning. "You better not be reading comics under the covers again. Or I swear..."

The voices and the lights ceased together almost immediately, right as she walked in. All she saw was Glenn on the bed, curled up and fast asleep.

***

Next morning was dull and previous night was left unmentioned when the kids left for school. Rachel duly finished her chores and rushed to find her car keys. Those at office won't pity her forever to cut her slack daily.

"Someone's looking motivated." Adam quipped, looking into her cubicle.

"I am tired." she rolled her eyes.

"Is it because you prepared the file overnight?"

"File?" asked Rachel.

"Report you were supposed to file today?" Adam answered.

"When I took two weeks off, I had no reports pending."

"Hello? The one I handed to you yesterday?"

"I didn't come yesterday, genius. Not funny."

"You… delivered the presentation yesterday… Are you okay?" Adam looked amused.

"Shut up. I went with my family for shopping."

"Uhh… you came here to work. Would you like to ask everyone else?"

"What's the date?" she enquired.

"6th"

"No, 5th, quit it." Rachel was alarmed now.

"Rachel… check your phone, and the office calendar."

As Rachel fumbled to check, confirm and validate the curious turn of events, her eyes bulged wider and wider. The sense of amusement was turning into a small terror. She sheepishly waved off Adam with an excuse, claiming it was her poor attempt at a prank. Then she went off to double check it on internet. Adam was right.

How did she lose an entire day? She came in AND delivered a presentation without her remembering anything. What is going on? Pain cannot make your memory weak so quickly, can it? Broken heart and brain… no that's a stretch.

***

Rest of the day was wasted in trying to forcibly dig through

125

the wall of memories with no result and before she realized, sun gave way to the darkness. She found herself already in her nightgown, surrounded by shadows and her eyes staring at the ceiling.

Her chain of thoughts threatened to unravel her mind until it was interrupted by a sound once again. Her brain paused, body froze and her ears perked up. It was a giggle.

Tim's? Not the time to be playing with toys. Glenn must have woken him up. She hopped off the bed and stormed towards the kids' rooms hoping to catch them in the act.

As she neared the doors, the whispers ceased yet again. She peaked into both rooms. Once more, the children were sleeping and she made sure they were indeed. Satisfied and disappointed, she proceeded to leave for her bedroom, just when her gaze fell on something.

The Kaleidoscope. It was lying at the feet of Tim's bed.

"Boys." she sighed, picked it up and packed it in the closet, in case someone walks and trips over it and cracks their head. She couldn't help but notice that the metallic toy was faintly warm. But then sleep intervened and no further thought was given to the matter.

***

"Listen, did any of you stayed up late playing toys? I am on to you."

"No." both replied in unison.

"Well good, because if I catch you, you are going to be in a lot of trouble."

"Never, mom." Glenn replied without looking up.

"And DO NOT leave it lying on the floor for someone to get hurt."

"I…I didn't."

"You better not, I picked it up from his room last night." she pointed at Tim.

"Sorry mom, I must have forgotten, I thought I put it under my pillow." Glenn answered.

"But I love simtree!!!" Tim happily exclaimed, pointing at the scope.

"What's that honey?" Rachel turned to Tim.

"Simtree! When you draw a line in cental of something both haffs look same same! Simtree!"

"Oohhh Symmetry? That's a big word, little sir. Who taught you that? Glenn?" Rachel laughed.

"No mom." Glenn rolled his eyes.

"Nooo, my friend simtree did."

"Is that right, your friend symmetry did?"

"Yesssss." He giggled.

Rachel smiled. How quickly children can forget trauma and bad memories. *No wonder they come up with imaginary friends to cope with tragedies.*

***

"Where were you?" Adam looked accusingly. "You were supposed to come early for the meeting today. Investors were not amused. Neither was Jane."

"What do you mean? Meeting was scheduled tomorrow!"

"Rachel, what is wrong with you? It was today!"

"I can't do this again. You said 8th." Rachel confronted him.

"And? Lady, seriously what is up with you? Look." Adam held up his phone.

Rachel felt her blood freeze as she saw the date. She pulled out her phone to confirm. "Not 7th?"

"No. God, no. I told you before you needed a longer break but you wouldn't listen."

"I am fine."

"No, you aren't. Please Rachel, just go home and I hate to say this…See your therapist. You have paid leaves left. Rest a bit. Come back when you are ok, because this is helping nobody. And what's with the table? Developed O.C.D. or something? You are THE clutter queen."

Rachel looked down and saw she had arranged the files into four stacks, a high stack of red files on top left and top right each and a smaller stack of blue files on both of the bottom corners of the table. Stationery arranged in center by height of pens.

"Nothing, I just wanted to see some symmetry."

"What was that, again?"

"Symme… Nothing." Rachel said, as confusion overwhelmed her.

"Go home Rachel." Adam said that as he walked away. Rachel was too horrified to argue. Clearly Adam too was trying to hold back his displeasure. But she had bigger worries.

Another day, gone. Erased from her memory. Lost in some dark pit. But… How? When did she clear her desk? She could not recall. Her trip back home was uneventful. She walked around as if in a drunken stupor or a person functioning without an iota of sleep. She put the kids to bed and then dropped into her own thoughts. Thinking. Thinking hard. She needs to see a doctor quickly, she decided. Her children depend on her.

The hour grew late and the clock's ticking grew louder. Yet sleep was nowhere near her. Tonight, everything seemed fine. No light. No sound. Just herself and her loss of memory. Having seen no breakthrough in her internal tussle with her brain, she decided to get up and take a walk around the house.

She checked up on the kids first, both sleeping soundly tonight. Good. Then she went downstairs without turning on any lights. Her body was by now habituated to the house and its obstacles. Darkness didn't bother her. She could sleepwalk her way around. As she passed by the den, an object slipped under her feet and she almost tripped.

A metallic cylindrical object. She felt it with fingers. "Hmm just as I expected. His Highness no longer needs his Kaleidoscope." She fiddled around with it, planning to take it back and hide it, only to give Glenn an earful when he came looking for it.

Rachel had barely taken few steps with it when something unexpected happened. The cylinder suddenly felt heavier. Hotter. Before she could register anything, it was faintly glowing and quickly heating up. The temperature and weight got to a point within seconds that her palms could not take it anymore and she dropped it on the floor.

She kept looking at the cylinder, now glowing in the dark, as it got brighter and brighter while the air around her got noticeably hotter. What happened next was a terrifying sight to behold. Millions of adventurers can live and die and not claim to have seen such a sight.

The Kaleidoscope was brightly glowing now and emitting a beam of light at the wall from its lens, almost like a flashlight.

The lit area on wall grew in size incredibly as it started forming a weird shape. Rachel kept looking at it mesmerized, terrified and frozen, all at once.

The shape grew and grew until it turned humanoid. While it was shaped liked a man; it was anything but. It was more of a human-ish projection on to thin air. But what was more incredible was that it had no features! The 'man' was devoid of any features like nose or eyelids or mouth even. Just an outline.

However, he was fully covered in beautiful reflective and multi-colored geometric patterns. Recursive multi-sided patterns, uncountable, formed by repetitive reflections of light. The colors, all the 7 hues of visible spectrum passing through a mirror. The patterns were arranged in perfect line symmetry!!!

Rachel screamed in terror as her fascination slowly got overwhelmed by horror, her senses returning and her blood flowing again. The creature took notice of the scream and turned around, preparing to pounce at her. This was enough for her poor heart, as she dropped to the floor, her senses dimming around her as she fainted.

***

Rachel woke up in her bed, drenched in sweat and with a nasty headache. She prayed she could lie down for few hours more, but that wasn't going to happen.
She reached her for her phone and warily checked the date. 11th.
'What? I lost TWO days? That can't be!'

Her mind ran with a million thoughts. 'It was just last night that I... That I what? Did something happen last night? I can't recall anything. I remember… gosh I remember the intense pain in my chest, the heat, the tiredness. But what from and why?'

Suddenly a concern hit her. "KIDS!!!!" She jumped and rushed to check on them. They were alone for two days. Rachel found them sleeping in their rooms and woke Glenn up.

"Mom it's FIVE am!" Glenn replied.

"First tell me what did we do yesterday?"

"You drove us to school because we missed the bus. Don't you remember?"

"Evening?"

"Mom, you are scaring me. We had takeout and we watched movies. You even let us stay up late."

"And day before yesterday?"

So apparently, she lived her life, she did her chores, she worked and she cared. Oddly, she didn't remember any of it. 'You need to see a doctor now, Rachel.' Her brain reminded her. Luckily, she got an appointment for the next week. All she needed to do now was survive and retain her much-dwindled sanity.

I keep losing time… I keep seeing lights… And I keep losing control over myself…

***

Thick smoke hung in air momentarily, a swirling mass of silver threads, gradually making its way up towards the ceiling. Those thin strands of smoke shined sharply under the yellow light bulb, the only source of light in the room. As the smoke snaked its way to the top, it kept getting dispersed by the slowly rotating blades of a lazy ceiling fan. The clock ticked cautiously, careful not to disrupt the suspense.

Mr. Wilkins sat in his chair, smoking, showered by dim yellow light in the dark warehouse. Rows of shelves and aisles melted into darkness. The gaping darkness swallowed everything save himself, the darkness being kept at bay by a solitary light bulb. It was a hot night and he sweat profusely, but he couldn't sleep tonight. He had been sitting there for so long that when he came to himself, he decided not to go home tonight and sleep in the office itself.

But that was not what was keeping him up. Whatever it was, was unsettling, bothersome, maddening; something stuck at the back of his head. Something that made him nervous and fearful. *Something sinister.*

He thought and thought harder, each time hitting a mental block. He was so deeply lost in thoughts that he couldn't even remember what was it he meant to ponder.

Ah, yes! The Kaleidoscope!

He had been uneasy since he had sold it. But why? He had no attachment to it.

Was it the pricing? Could he had made better profit, had he seen an expert and obtained a value appraisal first?

No! That's not it. This is more about fear, this was a feeling of dread, like when someone you love is in danger. He lit another cigarette.

Why could he not recall where he got the kaleidoscope from? Why such an intense feeling of dread over something so mundane, an act so trivial, a family so distant?

Is the Kaleidoscope that evil? He hadn't seen any proof. He didn't even know it existed in his possession! And no mishaps or oddity had happened.

Yet his heart beat fast, more so tonight than previous nights. His gut coiled within like he had been kicked. It has to be evil. 'Think harder, Wilkins.'

After some more minutes and cigarettes, he got up. He had some recollections return to him and he was terrified. No! What has he done? He must help them! Help them, how? He didn't know. Why? He couldn't answer. Maybe he didn't want the guilt, maybe he was terrified of being blamed if something happened.

He looked at his watch. 3.20 A.M. It was too late. That's a highly inappropriate timing to bother someone.

Maybe tomorrow. His brain rationalized.

NOW!!! His gut screamed.

Moments later a car hit the road and was hastily rushing out of the town toward Rachel's house.

***

The night drew quickly and Rachel reached her room with wobbly legs and a splitting headache. But sleep evaded her tired body once again, so she lay motionless, gazing at the ceiling. Hours rushed by silently, like a summer breeze and she lost the track of time and her thoughts.

Suddenly, without a warning came a soft sound. She heard it clearly. A conversation. She got up and marched towards the source, unmindful of personal safety, too tired to bother with second thoughts, careless of obstacles in the dark, determined to scream at the offending child.

She reached the two bedrooms, and the fleeting flashes of

light under the door betrayed the offender. So, it is Tim. Furious, she opened the door and barged in unceremoniously.

This turned out to be an extremely unwise decision as her brain started waking up and registering the ethereal scenery that greeted her. She felt the room being slightly warmer and brighter than usual. That was when she turned towards the bed.

There, a figure stooped over Tim, a faceless figure, a featureless figure, but formed like a human.

The tall figure radiated bright light and immense heat.

As her eyes adjusted to a sudden shift from pitch black to nearly blinding light, she noted the figure's skin was a pattern of repeating, unending geometric figures.

All intersecting, repetitive and colorful. The colors were all the hues that constituted the light, just like when the prism split them, she remembered that from school.

Just like the view from a Kaleidoscope.

The figure turned to her and viewed her curiously, inspecting her.

Then, slowly it started fading, never removing its gaze and peering straight through to her soul.

The thing just faded, then faded more and while it faded, the room grew cooler and darker.

Now standing alone in darkness once more, Rachel unfroze as her senses recovered and then screamed, which woke Tim up and sent him into a crying fit just as a breathless Glenn came running.

"Mom! What's wrong?"

"Glenn, get your jacket and shoes."

"But it's 4.30 a.m." he replied, half asleep.

"Glenn, get your shoes. WE ARE LEAVING. Right. Now."

A Late Night Fright

****

The darkness of the night hadn't faded yet. It was not yet time for the sunlight to peak over the horizon. The world stood silent. There was no breeze but cold air hung in the atmosphere. Not a living soul in sight, save for occasional chirping of some very early birds. Everyone slept in the young morning's tender embrace, except Rachel and her children.

The door flew open as a disheveled Rachel emerged. "I am getting the car, you hold Tim, and stand her by the door. DO. NOT. MOVE." Glenn nodded while a dazed Tim tried hard to not fall asleep. Rachel quickly brought the car right up to the front door.

"Get in. Hurry. Help get Tim into his seat and check the belt. Where are his medicines?" She rushed back inside as she remembered. She had some thoughts of fear, but a mother's instinct is stronger. She spotted the inhaler and the medicines by the kitchen counter.

She turned to leave, but a faint sound in the dark corridor drew her attention. She peered into darkness as a repetitive metallic faint sound kept getting closer and louder.
A metal cylinder rolled into her sight and stopped at her feet.
The Kaleidoscope!
She didn't think much of it. The kids must have misplaced it again. It must have rolled off from the table or maybe the staircase. Glenn probably dropped it in a hurry.

But the noise did test her alertness. Now jolted back to her senses, she made a dash back to the door, not waiting for any more surprises. Rachel returned to see Glenn struggling to strap Tim at the seat. She ran up to the driver's side, bent over to properly secure Tim. "There. Now we… Glenn? Glenn?!?!" she yelled as she watched Glenn walking back inside.

"One moment mom, my Kaleidoscope."

Rachel's heart skipped a beat. She got out and ran, terrified and determined.

She saw Glenn pick up the toy and turn to her.

The time felt like it slowed down.

And the door slammed shut in her face!

"Gleeeennn!!!!!!" Her heart wrenching, blood curdling scream pierced the veil of darkness and echoed in the house.

"My baby!" she screamed, shaking the elements of the night out of their slumber.

Instantly a light flashed from under the door.

The familiar hues spilled into the world outside, brightening it.

And then from the windows.

Finally, from the wooden boards too.

The intensity grew and grew until it was blinding, forcing her to shield her face.

The entire house grew brighter until it was bright as a sun on a hot summer afternoon.

She could feel the warmth of the light as it turned hotter. Soon it felt like standing near a furnace. However, it all stopped as quickly as it started. All over, like nothing ever happened.

The door flew open by itself.

"Glenn?" she called out, terrified and full of hope.

But there was no Glenn.

That Kaleidoscope. Is that it? The patterns, the lights, the colorful… thing, all looked like the ones created by that toy. Can a simple toy cause all this? Things did indeed start after she bought it home, or rather Glenn did. And Glenn was gone now.

She now realized, perhaps a bit too late. It was never going to let them go. It didn't even let her get too far.

So, is she condemned to live like this? Haunted, controlled and terrorized by a monstrous entity of lights and patterns? To live with dread, grief, questions, confusion and guilt?

***

Rachel cried bitterly, trying to regain her breath, as she sat on the ground weakened by sorrow and blinded by tears. Her mind had shut down and she felt no fear and no panic. She sat weeping, begging for Glenn but her heart knew he was gone. She finally got up, recollected her strength and halfheartedly she walked inside, holding fast to hope that her son might still be inside.

The house was still mildly warm. She took a few steps inside, cautious but not fearful, still calling out Glenn's name. There was no response.

Rachel then made her way towards the stairs and glanced up. Nothing. She slowly made her way upstairs. She was only halfway through the staircase, when something happened.

Sharp beams of yellow light poured into her house from doors and windows, and then slowly scanned down from their highest reach to downward.

As they reached the lowest point, they stopped moving but started getting intense.

Tim!

Terrified and angered at her idiocy, she ran down. Not again. Not him. God, please no. She doesn't deserve to be a mother. She ran to the door and stopped, out of breath.

The car was brightly lit. In the car was Tim, again nodding off unawares.

But something was very different. This was not the multicolored hot light she saw just now. This one was yellow and gold. And it came from behind the car.

She moved to inquire, and saw a car in her driveway coming to a halt.

Alarmed she yelled "Who is it? Hello?"

"Rachel it's me, Wilkins!"

"Mr. Wilkins? What are you doing here? Do you even know the time?"

"Rachel, I am so very sorry but I had a very bad feeling tonight, there is something you should know."

"There is no time, it can wait, I need your help." Rachel narrated her travails.

"I…I do not know what to say," Wilkins repeated, horrified and sheepish. "I will help you look for him."

***

Both of them re-entered the silent house, Rachel tightly clutching Tim to her chest who was too sleepy and confused to question. Finding Glenn was the only priority now. They walked through the den and kitchen, checked the entire ground floor. Nothing.

"Rachel, I am so sorry I didn't mean to. Sorry, I didn't tell you before."

"Sorry? What for?"

"For all of this." Wilkins answered.

"Wait, did you do this?" she asked.

"Do what? I didn't put you in harm's way knowingly."

"Where is my son?" she angrily demanded.

"I don't know, I just don't. I wish I did."

"You are lying. You took my son. You did this."

"I didn't do anything to you, Rachel. I am here for the… *Kaleidoscope*…"

Rachel paused and looked at him.

"You mean you knew it was not right and you still gave it to me?" Rachel asked, her face turning red.

"No! I didn't remember. It… does things to you… To your memory. To your loved ones. It takes over you."

Rachel's expressions hardened. Her fists secretly clenched and she bit her lips.

"I swear, If I remembered it does these things, Rachel, I would have never…"

"I would have never sacrificed your kid?" She replied angrily and sarcastically.

"It took Glenn… I am sorry… It takes your loved ones… My wife… My daughter… They didn't go missing during vacations…" Now Wilkins teared up.

"You have got to help me find him, it's your mess."

"We can try, but Glenn is gone, and it will come for Tim and it will win. You can't run. Then it will move on from you to someone else." Wilkins said, utterly defeated.

"Don't you dare give me that. The children are my life."

"Rachel…" Wilkins pleaded.

***

They had reached the stair landing now and were looking

straight down the corridor towards the children's bedrooms. Their last and most plausible shot, though Wilkins knew better.

They decided to go to Tim's room first. Empty. Silent and dark. The playful watchfulness and the stillness in the room was unnerving. It almost felt like someone was watching them, even though it was empty. They hastily shut the door and walked towards Glenn's room. At this point they were not sure what they were looking for, what they expected to find or how they planned to deal with anything they found.

Next, they entered Glenn's room. As expected, it was empty, but Rachel was not giving up on her son that easily. They looked around the room. They didn't find any sign of Glenn, but tucked neatly among the clothes inside the closet was the Kaleidoscope. Rachel scooped it up in anger, unmindful of danger.

Wilkins turned his gaze to it, and his fears returned along with the painful memories. He started sweating profusely.

"You should not be holding that." he warned.

"This thing has my kid; how do we get him back?" Rachel said, examining it.

Wilkins had no heart to remind her once more about the inevitable truth, no one comes back.

In that very moment, it happened once more. Having lured them into the ambush laid for its final three victims, the nefarious being of light sprung the trap they had walked into.

A faint glow started emitting from the Kaleidoscope, beckoning the return of an all too familiar entity, a phenomenon both of them knew dearly. The glow gently grew brighter and brighter and the temperature shot up like a hot kettle on stove. Eventually it became unbearable and Rachel dropped it, which made matters instantly worse. It glowed as if a thousand suns exploded at once. Blinding light bathed the surroundings.

Wilkins was mortified at the sight, but fighting through his terror, he managed to croak a few words of warning "What are you doing, are you insane? Run."

Rachel knew what she must do. She grabbed Tim tightly and felt for the doorway.

"Rachel, run!" he begged, struggling to run to safety right behind her.

Rachel felt her path, all the way to the corridor. Finally, her pupils relaxed a little and adjusted to dark. She then broke into a mad rush, as she skipped stairs and hopped through the door. Without wasting any time, she madly ran to the car and within a few seconds she had strapped Tim securely and was in the driver's seat. She looked on intently at the open door.

Wilkins didn't come out. She looked on, towards the empty dark patch that was her door, peering inside hoping to see something. She didn't see Wilkins but a brightness was lighting up inner corridors, just faintly enough to look like someone had left a small bulb on. It grew brighter and shadows made by the rails of staircases imprinted on the lower wall like someone walking down with a flashlight. She knew what it meant. She knew what was coming.

She started her car and hit the road immediately.

***

Rachel drove fast, never looking back. There were no houses nearby to witness anything between the forest and the grassy field. The house looked ominous even from this distance. The light from the house shot up into sky and poured into the surroundings. They went up the sky like a colorful searchlight, and filtered through very dense vegetation. She could still see bright flashes from the house but the distance was growing as car sped further away.

'Wonder what's going on there now?' She should be going back. But her heart said no. She had to protect Tim. But Glenn… She was screaming inside. It was the most cowardly thing she could have done. She left her child behind; no mother will ever do that. Yet, she had to, because Tim needed her. He needed safety. She also knew what empty house had meant, when she went to look for Glenn. She consoled herself by looking at Tim. This was not a time to stop and grieve, that time will come. There is an entire lifetime ahead for her guilt and grief to attack her.

She was so lost in her thoughts that her heart nearly stopped when 'that' sound came. It was an extremely loud boom. Her head quickly turned around and she looked across the field. The house! The house had exploded!

The explosion sent a trillion bright sparks in the air. Plethora of colorful pieces shot out into the sky like firecrackers. She could make out pieces of debris falling far and wide as a fire started and engulfed all that remained. Her dreams shattered, falling like rain but in the form of small embers. Her dream place where she was supposed to have nursed her broken heart, gone.

***

The car raced down the desolate road, Rachel feeling the cold dry wind of early dark morning slap her repeatedly into attention. Her body was feeling a million things at once. She was replaying the night's events and memories over and over again.

One memory however, was particularly lodged in her brain.

"You mean you knew it was not right and you still gave it to me?" Rachel asked, her face turning red.

"No! I didn't remember. It... does things to you... To your memory. To your loved ones. It takes over you." Rachel's expressions hardened. Her fists secretly clenched and she bit her lips.

"I swear, If I remembered it does these things, Rachel, I would have never..."

"I would have never sacrificed your kid?" She replied angrily and sarcastically.

Rachel thought about it again. How furious she felt. The rage. The anger that overcame her. Her baby was gone and all because of Wilkins. He stole her one chance at happiness.

"What are you doing, are you insane? Run," he yelled. "Rachel, Run!" These were the last words he uttered to her in that room, out of concern for her. But were they?

Her fingers grasped the steering wheel tightly as she thought about it more. She remembered how her rage had replaced her fear and self-preservation. She remembered how she ran out of the room and turned around. She had stopped at the door to Glenn's room, her eyes meeting that of terrified Wilkins running just behind her.

She recalled how she pushed him back and shut the door on him without a second thought. Without remorse.

"Rachel? Rachel!" He had screamed in terror.

"Rachel, open up." As his sweaty fists banged the door.

"Rachel, help me!" And then his screams of fear turned into those of pain and agony.

"Mommy, where is Glenn?" Tim now wide awake, asked.

"He will come later, sweety. I promise." Rachel replied, wiping her tears.

"But where are we going?"

"Far away, honey. Far, far away from here."

With this, she stepped on the accelerator, and the car gained momentum, leaving a gentle puff of dust behind on the gravel. The engine hummed louder and, in that noise, the faint rattling of a lone *metallic cylinder* rolling from vibrations, emanating from under the backseat went unnoticed…

***

The car sped on the dark empty road as Rachel zoned in and out with panic, fear, numbness and disbelief on her recent actions. The fact that car still was on the road was a miracle. Tim had been crying till the sleep got him. It was just her and the eerie silence of a frozen dark morning. She had no time to rethink or to cry. She needed to get away from this nightmare.

She looked out to the horizon as she saw the world in slumber, unawares of her plight. She cursed them silently. She was getting irritable now, sweaty and angry for reasons well founded. But she kept driving. She kept thinking over the events of the night and she kept muttering profanities.

Tim gently woke up again, rubbing his eyes. "Mom, where is Glenn?"

She didn't have the heart to answer him. "He went back to sleep, honey. We will see him in afternoon." Satisfied but restless, Tim got busy again, fidgeting with the seatbelt and trying to stay awake. Then he giggled.

He picked up the Kaleidoscope from under the seat.

Rachel, attracted by the giggle, looked into the rear-view mirror and her eyes bulged due to terror and incredulity.

"Where did that come from?" she enquired with horror.

"Simtree gave it. Look!"

Rachel's heart skipped a beat; a renewed wave of terror gripped her. Sweat appeared on her brow. She fiddled with the steering and turned around.

"Tim, put it back!" She could feel her arms going weak. Too late!

The Kaleidoscope was glowing once again. Dimly at first, like a weak flashlight and then got brighter progressively. The light enveloped them, but it wasn't painful. This heat didn't hurt. It was bittersweet; soothing actually. The panic of that car's occupants had turned into silence and acceptance.

An unmeasured amount of time sped past, and no one could tell whether it was moments or hours. Was the car even running anymore? Vibrantly colored light glowed with geometric figures in them, filling their minds with repeated, cyclic designs.

Recursive fractal designs with variegated colors. Infinite reflections of new patterns intersecting over and over again.

It beckoned Rachel, invited her. Such soothing feeling after all the pain she had been through lately. All her sorrow, gone; vanished into the depth of those repeating patterns, locked away behind those colors, and permanently too, if she so desired.

Her trance-like dreams and thoughts suddenly vanished, her mind pulled into reality by violent jerking and harsh crunching noises as her car rushed through the vegetation uncontrollably. The luck had finally run out and her car, unsupervised, left the road and entered the thick bushes to her right, never slowing.

The car crushed the plants, miraculously avoiding the rails and thick trees, and kept rolling down the slope, forever entering the depths of thick growth. The slide continued for a pretty minute after she hit the brakes, before finally coming to a halt. The crash site was masked from road by the canopy of dark leaves and a screen of trees behind her.

Rachel stumbled out of the wreck, her head spinning, as she looked around. No one was going to find her this deep into nowhere. There was no trail behind her to attract attention, no human, no civilization that could by luck render assistance, no clear trail of destruction. She will have to walk back with Tim. She checked him. He was still strapped to the seat and perfectly okay.

Before she could start, a gust of wind hit her. She turned away to shield herself but spotted something new in the process. A faint light was visible, coming from behind the trees at some distance. Perhaps a small cabin? Or a camp? Anything was greatly welcome. She started walking towards it. After a brisk walk she arrived at her destination.

It was a bed of light. A sheet of light spread across a vast expanse on the ground. Calm and gentle. Rachel was instantly mesmerized. Past events of this very night should have cautioned her. But no, instead she felt pulled to it. Hypnotized, she marched towards it.

The giant glowing mass of light was swirling now, always on the ground, with finite boundaries and clearly defined distinction between the forest floor and the bed of light. As she got closer, she saw a dark pattern emerge. It was tiny at first, it grew and dissolved into itself, leaving a ripple of many colors behind.

Then the process repeated again and again, with ripples dancing in all directions. The rest of the sheet of light started turning from white to heterochromatic. Each generated color produced geometric patterns which were rotating, swirling, growing and producing more patterns within themselves.

Entire area soon turned kaleidoscopic. Plethora of designs and infinite reflections in a multi-hued carnival. All dancing in circles as if they had a mind of their own. *It was like looking through a giant kaleidoscope.* The dark circular pattern in middle continued to shoot out multicolored ripples.

Rachel was spellbound. There were no more thoughts left in her mind, neither care, nor fear. She continued walking, aiming to reach the dark moving circle with many lights in the middle. The progenitor of these patterns and colors. Her means to an end. The answer to her pain.

She kept walking. Making her way through, as infinitely repetitive patterns gave way to her body, each pattern dancing around her. Every pattern in vicinity looked so small, but also large at the same moment, as they directly ingrained her brain with delightful imageries. The ripples reached her body now. She was getting closer to her destination.

When Rachel reached the center, the black circle containing the mass of colorful lights and a hotbed of mathematical symmetries, yet not devoid of motion, surrounded her. It tugged at her, pulled her waist, like a naughty child begging for mother's attention. She accepted and let herself go as the mass climbed her, first her chest and then her neck.
The patterns danced faster now, and it all entered her eyes like a very bright television in the middle of night.
Any moment it would take her, relieve her of her past. That's all she wants.

The layer of patterns was up to her face, and neared her eyes. The warm grip, the chill down her spine. *Soon.*

It covered her as she gasped for breath. Her body thrashed violently while she was being pulled. The thrashing made the patterns subside, leaving behind a dark form, a large body of water. No sheet of lights. No façade on display.

Just the lake.

She came to herself. Her trance ended swiftly. This isn't what she wanted. Rachel thrashed even more violently, as her lungs burned for the want of air. As she was going underwater, she thought about her son. Her mission. Her duty. Her treasure.

Tim.

She had left him in the car, alone, hurt and lost.

Rachel screamed as she went under water, losing the battle, releasing only air bubbles.

The last sight she saw was nothing but a cold dark curtain of the lake's surface, as the disturbance from her thrashing in the water resettled.

Her eyes closed forever.

And there was no other color or pattern in attendance. Only the darkness.

***

"This is a total mess."

"Well, what do you think?" asked the second policeman.

"I don't want to think about it. I don't even know where to begin." First policeman replied.

"The house is an even bigger mess. We would be lucky if we found something out of the debris."

"Then there is him," The first policeman pointed to Tim, being attended to by a medic. "Why would the mother do that?"

"Beats me. Lucky us, we found him when we did. I don't

know how he made through all of this, two days all by himself." Second policeman answered, pointing to a child happily chatting with the medics.

They looked at Tim and waved. Tim turned around quickly to face them and with a big smile, he waved back. They did not notice him holding, in his tiny hands, a small shiny toy.
A *Kaleidoscope.*

Acknowledgements

This book was made possible due to the constant support from an army of well-wishers standing behind me.

First of all, huge thanks to my sister whose indispensable help made the very writing of this book possible. Forever indebted.

A note of thanks to my cousins, my aunts and my family who constantly encouraged me.

A very special thanks to Sarah, who held me hostage until I finished the book. It made all the difference.
Big thanks to Alina, my best friend, for hyping me up way too much and being there when I needed help.
I made sure to haunt you both in my stories.
Thanks to Anderlyn, a trusted friend, for her absolutely crucial last minute assistance.

Grateful to the host of online friends, who boosted my confidence, gave their views and helped me promote.

To everyone else, who stood with me during my darkest times.

Stories Author Loves To Read On Repeat

- **H. P. Lovecraft:** The Call Of Cthulhu, The Color Out Of Space, At The Mountains Of Madness, The Lurking Fear, The Dunwich Horror, The Lurking Fear, The Shadow Over Innsmouth, The Shadow Out Of Time, The Whisperer In The Darkness
- **Sarah Demens:** Uncanny Series: Book 1 - Welcome To Hollowgrove and Book 2 - Belief Is Half The Battle
- **Edith Wharton:** The Ghost Stories of Edith Wharton
- **Edgar Allan Poe:** The Black Cat, The Gold-Bug, The Fall Of The House Of Usher, The Pit And The Pendulum, The Masque Of Red Death, The Facts In The Case Of M. Valdemar, The Raven, The Tell-Tale Heart
- **Mary Shelley:** Frankenstein
- **Bram Stroker:** Dracula
- **Susan Hill:** The Woman In Black
- **Josh Malerman:** Bird Box
- **Stephen King:** Pet Sematary
- **Short Horror Story Collection:** 666 The Number Of The Beast
- **Arthur Conan Doyle:** The Best Supernatural Tales of Arthur Conan Doyle

A LATE NIGHT FRIGHT: TALES OF HORROR AND MACABRE

- Also available in E-book, Paperback and Hardcover formats across select Amazon marketplaces and other online retailers globally.
- Paperback available in India on Notion Press website.